When Jen got home she hurried up to her room and got ready for bed. She then stood at the window, looking over at Dawson's house. She saw Dawson, Pacey, and Andie laughing about something. Good—Joey wasn't there.

No, wait. There she was. Jen's heart sank. Of course, Joey would say they were just friends hanging out and watching a movie.

Something twisted in Jen's heart. She knew what she wanted—to be loved by Dawson, purely, with all his heart, no matter what her past.

But he loved Joey.

"Jennifer, is that you?" her grandmother called. "Come downstairs, I have the best news."

Jen sighed but went downstairs to join her grandmother, who handed her a glass of juice as soon as she entered the kitchen.

"Guess who's coming to visit?" her grandmother asked.

"From the look on your face, someone you like. Which worries me, frankly."

"Our visitor is your cousin Courtney!"

Jen set down her glass of juice. "The Cousin From Hell is coming *here*?"

Dawson's Creek™
Trouble in Paradise

Based on the television series "Dawson's Creek"™
created by **Kevin Williamson**

Written by C. J. Anders

POCKET BOOKS
New York   London   Toronto   Sydney   Tokyo   Singapore

An *Original* Publication of POCKET BOOKS

POCKET BOOKS, a division of Simon & Schuster Inc.
1230 Avenue of the Americas, New York, NY 10020

ISBN: 0-671-03527-4

First Pocket Books printing June 1999

10 9 8 7 6 5 4 3 2

POCKET and colophon are registered trademarks of Simon & Schuster Inc.

DAWSON'S CREEK is a registered trademark of Columbia TriStar Television, Inc.

Printed in the U.S.A.

To the fans of Sam, Emma, and Carrie; Jane, Kimmy, Sandra, and Savy; Cisco, Nicole, and Melody; Chelsea, Karma, and Lisha; Cindy, Tina Wu, and Veronica; Katie and Lisa and Cindy and Pepper and The Virus; Erin, Tara, and Noelle; Paris, Lexi, and Juliet; Darcy, Amber, Patsi, and especially Lara Ardeche . . . we remain fans of yours.

Trouble in Paradise

Chapter 1

Jen Lindley walked into the Ice House just as a bunch of raucous college-age guys were on their way out.

"Whoa! Worlds collide!" the guy in the front of the pack whooped. He tried to feint around Jen but bumped into her, practically knocking her over. She lost her balance and would have fallen if not for a pair of strong arms that caught her. Meanwhile, the guy who had almost knocked her over continued out the door without a backward glance.

"You okay?" Strong Arms asked.

Jen righted herself and checked him out. His hunky arms were attached to an equally hunky torso, which was attached to a Ryan Phillippe-esque face.

"Your friend's a jerk," Jen told him.

"He's a friend of a friend," Strong Arms said. "My

real friends are only semi-jerks." He grinned at her. "I'm Drake Keller. You're—?"

"Jen Lindley."

"Jen Lindley," he repeated, still grinning. "I think this is what is commonly known as 'meeting cute.' So, do you live here or—"

"Yo, Keller, let's go, man!" One of his friends had stuck his head inside the door. "We're already late."

"Be right there." Drake turned back to Jen. "Well, I guess this is boy meets girl, boy loses girl. Anyway, I apologize for my friend of a friend."

"Apology accepted," Jen said. "Nice meeting you." She watched him walk away. He looked just as good going as he had coming.

"As we used to so cleverly say in grade school, take a picture, it'll last longer," Joey Potter called to Jen as she sailed by. She carried a platter loaded with plates of burgers and fries.

"Forget it," Jen mumbled. "Guys that cute are dangerous." She'd been in trouble with cute guys one too many times.

It was an unusually warm summer night for Capeside, Massachusetts, and Jen had been home alone, monumentally bored. So she'd wandered next door to Dawson's, to see what he was up to. Dawson's dad was in the garage, sorting through his golf clubs. He said he thought Dawson had gone to the Ice House.

The Ice House. Joey's sister Bessie owned it, and Joey was waitressing there all summer. Though Jen and Dawson had been a couple briefly, it was patently obvious to Jen and everyone else that Dawson was still in love with Joey. So Jen and Dawson had broken up. Jen knew she should get over him. Move on. But her stupid heart refused to listen to her head.

Jen looked over at Joey, who was delivering the burger platters to a table of young girls. Joey was tall and fresh-looking, beautiful in a natural way of which she seemed completely unaware. Jen tried to remember when she, too, had been that innocent, but her memory didn't go back that far.

She spied Dawson sitting at the counter with his best friend, Pacey Witter, and Pacey's girlfriend, Andie McPhee. Jen walked over and heard them arguing about something.

"You're completely wrong," Dawson was saying to Andie. "To even compare the film of *Man of La Mancha* to the film of *Don Quixote* is to totally trivialize Cervantes' work."

"Sue me, I like musicals," Andie said, swiping a French fry from Pacey's plate.

"Gee, Dawson, the category is movies, *quelle surprise,*" Jen joked, settling onto the stool next to him.

"Hey, Jen," Dawson greeted her. "I rented the 1957 Russian version of *Don Quixote* to watch tonight, and Andie's sublimating her anger with French fries because I didn't get *Man of La Mancha* instead."

"It has subtitles, Dawson. Movies with subtitles should be illegal in the summertime," Pacey decreed. "Too much work."

"This happens to be a seminal piece of filmmaking," Dawson insisted.

"Not every film experience has to be important, Dawson," Andie said.

"I think I can settle this little dispute," Jen broke in. "It's a sultry summer night. As teenagers, it's thus our responsibility to be doing wild and sultry things."

"Preferably while wearing very little clothing," Pacey added.

"Exactly," Jen agreed. "Which leaves out all movies, case closed, and you'll get my bill in the mail." She took a sip of Dawson's milk shake.

"So young and yet so profound," Pacey approved. He reached for a button on his shirt. "Shall we shed?"

"We shall shed-up," Andie quipped sweetly.

Joey came up behind them. "My feelings exactly." She dropped a bus tray of dirty dishes on the counter and eyed Jen warily. "Please tell me you don't want to order."

"Take a break, Joey, I'll mooch Dawson's milk shake."

"Mooch away," Dawson offered.

Jen winked at him, and her heart raced when he smiled back. Why did he still get to her so much? After all, she was the sophisticated one, the been-there-done-that queen of the fast lane who had moved to tiny Capeside from New York City. So how could one Capeside guy who dreamed of becoming the next Steven Spielberg turn her into mush?

Maybe, Jen thought, if Dawson and Joey were still officially an item she could force her heart to play dead. Her own feelings totally confused her. Sometimes she wanted Dawson desperately, other times she wasn't so sure. But Jen was always sure of this:

when Dawson looked at Joey, and she could see how much he still loved Joey, Jen hurt in a way she tried not to expose too often.

Dawson's love was just so . . . so pure, Jen mused. Immature, maybe. Idealistic, definitely. And yet she missed it. So much.

Bessie carried a freshly baked carrot cake out from the kitchen. "Did you check on that table of girls in the back, Joey?"

"We bonded like sisters," Joey told her sarcastically, reaching under the plastic dome on the counter for a jelly doughnut. "They told me they're from Boston, and they're thirteen going on seven. They want to know where they can go to party with hot guys."

"See, this is exactly why we won't live in a big city," Bessie said, heading back into the kitchen.

Jen craned her neck to look at the girls. Two of them were smoking, desperately trying to look sophisticated. "They remind me of me at that age."

One of the girls got up and walked toward them. She had long red hair and freckles she'd tried to cover with too much makeup. A lit cigarette dangled from one hand. "Hey, what's happening?" she asked them, exhaling smoke.

Andie waved the smoke away. "This is the nonsmoking area."

"Whatever," the girl said nastily. "So, any hot parties tonight?"

"Sorry," Pacey said. "They were all last night."

The girl shook her hair off her face. "No offense, but this town sucks. Do you guys know how we can score some beers without ID?"

"You might be a little young for that," Jen said.

The girl's face turned bright red. "Who are you supposed to be, my mother?"

"I just mean I've been there," Jen said softly. "It's not worth it."

"Get a life," the girl spat, and whirled away.

"God, kids get into stuff young now, huh?" Andie marveled. "I was playing with Barbie dolls at her age."

"It's sad," Dawson said. "She's already bypassed romantic innocence and moved on to meaningless lust."

"Watch it," Pacey cautioned. "I happen to find lust very meaningful."

"You know what I mean, Pacey," Dawson insisted. "Like, take *Don Quixote* for instance."

Andie groaned and dropped her head on the counter.

"He loved Dulcinea so much that he only saw her as perfect and beautiful," Dawson went on, "no matter how anyone else saw her, no matter what she did."

"Dawson, I hate to be the one to burst your romantic bubble, but Dulcinea had sex for money," Jen said, as Joey started to wipe down the counter. "With everybody."

"That's my point. To him, Dulcinea was still pure, no matter what she did."

Jen chuckled. "Wait, Dawson. Aren't you the guy who went ballistic when his girlfriend kissed another guy?"

"*Former* girlfriend," Joey added quickly, a little embarrassed, since Jen was referring to her.

"At the time, you weren't 'former,' " Jen reminded her.

"Pre-commitment, everything is forgiven," Dawson explained. "Post-commitment is entirely different."

"You're hopelessly romantic, Dawson," Andie said.

"Or just plain hopeless," Joey teased. "Tilting at windmills like Don Quixote, madly in love with love."

"Tease all you like," Dawson said good-naturedly. "I think the world needs more romance, not less."

"Well then, you'll be thrilled to know that true romance is coming to Capeside," Jen told him.

Dawson cocked his head at her. "Does an explanation follow that statement?"

"Could be," Jen said. "Joey, do you still have that little portable TV in the kitchen?"

"Yeah, I guess," Joey said. "Why?"

Jen checked her watch. "So that we can watch Dawson's mom on the local evening news in exactly five minutes."

"Gee, Jen, I love my mom, but I really do see plenty of her at home," Dawson said, polishing off another fry.

"It just so happens that I sort of interned for your mom at the TV station today," Jen told him.

"That's great, Jen."

She smiled sheepishly. "Well, you're the one who got me started on this producing thing. Anyway, I was there when she did her remote this afternoon. You really need to see it."

Joey rolled her eyes but got the TV from the

kitchen. "This thing is older than I am," she said, plugging it in, "so I have no idea if it still works."

She turned to the right channel, and a shot of Dawson's mom, Gale Leery, filled the screen. She was standing in front of Capeside's modest city hall. Joey turned the sound up.

"I'm here with Marsha O'Brien, director of the Capeside Tourism Bureau," Gale said. She turned to a middle-aged woman in a blue suit. "Marsha, I understand that the city council has exciting news for us."

"That's right, Gale," Marsha said. "We know that Capeside is one of the most romantic locations in America, and now the whole world is going to know about it. I'm pleased to announce the first annual summer Capeside Romance Festival, which will take place the weekend of June twenty-eighth and -ninth."

"Capeside Romance Festival?" Dawson echoed incredulously. "Whose brilliantly tacky concept was that?"

"Shhh," Jen hissed.

"Tell us more," Dawson's mother urged.

"Well, Gale," Marsha gushed, "our slogan is 'Capeside *Is* Romance.' "

Dawson laughed. "That reeks!"

"There'll be something for everyone," Marsha went on, "including a costume parade of great lovers, with prizes for best costume, and a contest for longest kiss. We're hoping to break the *Guinness Book of World Records* on that one!"

"Sounds exciting," Gale said.

"Sounds excruciating," Dawson quipped.

"We think so," Marsha agreed. "Many merchants have donated wonderful prizes, and a press release has gone out to travel agents across the country. We don't have a lot of lead time to get the festival together, so we're counting on everyone to pitch in. Remember: Capeside *is* romance."

Dawson's mom turned to the camera. "There you have it, folks. Romance is coming to Capeside, complete with the world's longest kiss. Back to you in the studio."

Joey clicked off the TV.

Jen looked at her friends. "So?"

"Hey, Capeside *is* romance," Pacey mocked.

"I think it sounds like fun," Andie decided.

"A romance festival is the opposite of romantic," Dawson said. "I mean, a *kissing contest*?"

Joey shook her head ruefully. "I ask myself, who would actually come to the Capeside Romance Festival? My mind draws a big, fat blank."

"Oh, I don't know," Jen said. "You guys fail to see Capeside's charm because you grew up here. But I see it."

"Let us know how it goes," Pacey said. "I'm thinking road trip for that weekend."

"Yeah?" Jen asked, all innocence. "Like, you'd never enter, say, the kissing contest, would you?"

"I'll be fishing on the Moose River in Maine," Pacey replied.

"Gee, what a shame," Jen shrugged. "Because the winning kissers get great prizes, like a gift certificate to Filene's department store—"

"Oh, now *that's* incentive," Pacey said sarcastically.

"—and use of a new Viper for one week," Jen added.

Pacey nearly fell off his stool. The Viper was his dream car, and Jen knew it. "Please tell me you aren't just toying with my lust for material objects," Pacey begged.

"It's on the press release," Jen told him. "Longest kissers get a fully loaded Viper to drive for one week. Gas paid."

Pacey's eyes slid over to Andie.

"Oh, no," she declared, folding her arms. "Forget it."

"But we can win," Pacey pleaded. "And I'd get a small taste of my dream vehicle come true."

"Dream on," Andie snorted.

"Hey, how about, like, a check!" the redheaded girl at the table in the back yelled to Joey.

"Hey, how about, like, you're obnoxious," Joey said under her breath, but headed for the table of girls.

"Be sure to invite them to the Romance Festival!" Pacey told Joey as she walked away.

"Actually," Dawson mused, "if the festival is a success, it could mean a lot of business for the Ice House, which would be nice for Bessie and Joey. Other than that, though, the concept is basically deadly."

"You might be interested in this, Dawson," Jen said. "There's also a contest for best short promo video about Capeside. The winning entry will be sent to travel agents all over the country."

He stared at her. "You couldn't possibly think such a thing would actually interest me, Jen."

She reached for his milk shake. "I couldn't?"

"Why would I want to make a commercial *travelogue*? The idea is repellent."

"Yeah, you're right," Jen agreed. She took a sip of his shake. "It's too bad, though, because the winning video is going to be buried in a special Capeside time capsule that won't be dug up until the new millennium."

"So what?" Dawson said. "That's in a matter of months."

"Oh, this would be the *next* millennium, Dawson," Jen explained. "You know. The year 2999."

Dawson thought a minute. "Wow. I can't say that idea is entirely without appeal," he admitted.

Jen smiled smugly. "Somehow I thought that's how you'd see it. Do I know my friends or do I know my friends?"

"An artist wants his or her work to live on," Dawson said defensively. "It's like . . . like creating a child."

"But not nearly as much fun," Pacey pointed out.

Joey tramped over to them and tossed her order to Dawson. "One female infant back there asked me to relay this message to you, Dawson, and I quote: 'You are cute. You have a cute butt. Do you want to party?' End quote."

"Are you serious?" Dawson looked over at the girls, who giggled and waved to him. "That's pathetic."

"I agree," Pacey said. "My butt is much cuter than Dawson's."

Andie punched him in the arm.

The giggling girls came over to them.

"So, did you get my message?" a skinny blond girl asked Dawson as light bounced off the braces in her mouth.

"How old are you, twelve?" he asked.

"Thirteen." She gave him a defiant look. "I've dated guys older than you, you know."

"That's not something to brag about," Dawson told her.

"Or very romantic," Jen added.

"Are you kidding?" the blond jeered. "Romance is, like, some stupid fairy-tale thing." She threw some money on the counter. "Let's go," she told her friends. "My mom's probably having a hissy fit."

The girls sauntered away, the skinny blond walking backward, eyes on Dawson. "You don't know what you just missed," she said, just before she opened the door.

Dawson shook his head ruefully. "I was just propositioned by a thirteen-year-old. I may have to rethink my entire reaction to this romance festival. Just possibly, anything that promotes love and romance is a good thing."

"Look at it this way, Dawson," Joey suggested. "If the Capeside Romance Festival is the abject failure that I anticipate it will be, next year we can have the Capeside Lust Festival. Those girls can bring all their friends."

"Someday I hope those girls experience real romance," Dawson said. "That makes all the difference."

Jen watched as Dawson and Joey shared meaningful eye contact. Sparks that weren't supposed to exist anymore flew. And they weren't flying toward her.

Jen got up. "Well, I'm outta here."

Dawson tore his eyes away from Joey. "Wait, Jen, do you want to come over and watch *Don Quixote?*"

"No thanks, Dawson. I think I've experienced just about all the real romance that I can handle in one night. Catch you later."

Jen left the Ice House and headed home, back to her grandmother's house. It was a gorgeous, clear night. That is, she thought, it would be gorgeous if you were wrapped in the arms of the guy you loved.

When she got home, she hurried up to her room, being in no mood to deal with her grandmother. They were getting along better these days, but sometimes her grandmother's moralistic, black-and-white view of the world was a little tough to take.

Jen got ready for bed, then stood at the window, looking over at Dawson's house. The light went on in his bedroom. She saw Dawson, Pacey, and Andie laughing about something. Good—Joey wasn't there.

No, wait. There she was. Jen's heart sank. Of course, Joey would say they were just hanging out, that it wasn't a "date," that she and Dawson weren't a couple, that they were just friends hanging out, watching *Don Quixote.*

Something twisted in Jen's heart. She knew what she wanted—to be Dawson's Dulcinea, loved by him, purely, with all his heart, no matter what her past.

But he loved Joey.

Jen knew she was dreaming the impossible dream.

"Jennifer, is that you?" her grandmother called upstairs. She had been in the kitchen when Jen had come in.

"Yeah, it's me, Grams," she called back dutifully while shaking her head. Who else would it be? Ever since her grandfather had died, her grandmother was even more protective of her than usual.

"Come downstairs and have some juice," Grams urged.

Jen sighed but went downstairs to join her grandmother, who handed her a glass of grape juice as soon as she came into the kitchen.

"I have the best news," Grams declared.

"Yeah?"

"Guess who's coming to visit?" her grandmother asked.

Jen took a long swallow of her juice and leaned against the counter. "From the look on your face, someone you like. Which worries me, frankly."

"Our visitor is your cousin Courtney!"

Jen set down her glass of juice. "The Cousin from Hell is coming *here*?"

"Shame on you, Jennifer," Grams chided. "Courtney is a lovely girl with perfect manners. She called and said that since you were kind enough to come to New York for her sweet sixteen party, she wants to return the favor and come to visit Capeside. Isn't that lovely?"

"Other than the fact that she's a lying, hypocritical, shallow, self-centered, back-biting witch, it's just ducky."

"Jennifer! She's family."

"Don't remind me," Jen said. "When is she arriving?"

"Next week," Grams said. "I had hoped you'd be as excited as I am."

"Sorry, Grams, you hoped wrong. I'm going to bed."

As Jen went upstairs, her mind reeled. Courtney the Perfect had to have some ulterior motive for coming to town.

The problem was, Jen had no idea what it could possibly be.

Chapter 2

Ryan Phillippe took Jen in his arms. "I've always loved you," he said huskily. "I don't know why I was so blind for so long." His lips came down on hers, his strong arms pulling her closer—

"Jen, wake up! Jen!"

Huh? Someone was shaking her out of the greatest dream, which was amazingly not about Dawson. She barely opened her eyes.

The real Dawson loomed over her.

Unless she was still dreaming.

"Dawson?" she squinted at the clock on her dresser. It was barely 6 A.M. "It's the middle of the night!"

"It's bright and early, Jen, and I know I'm a cretin to wake you up, but I had to tell you."

She sat up a little. "What?" she asked groggily.

"You know that for an entire week now I've been

trying to come up with an approach for the Cape-side video contest, but every idea seemed so hackneyed, overused—"

"Cut to the chase, Dawson," Jen croaked. "I need at least three more hours of shut-eye."

"Right. Sorry. Okay, here it is. *Don and Dulcie.*"

Jen blinked. "You want to run that by me again?"

"My film will be about a modern teenage Don Quixote searching for his Dulcinea in Capeside," Dawson explained, his eyes shining with excitement. "I'll get in all the sites that would entice tourists, but they'll fall in love with the town almost peripherally as they fall in love with the love story. So, what do you think?"

"It has potential," Jen decided. "After I wake up."

"Great. Then you'll be my producer again."

Jen laughed. "I will?"

"I'm hoping you will," Dawson amended. "How's that?"

"You might have a shot," she admitted.

"Great," he said again, thrusting some pages at her. "A first draft. I was up most of the night writing it."

Jen eyed him warily. "This isn't another thinly veiled autobiography like *Creek Daze* was, is it? You know, Dawson Leery as Don Quixote, Joey Potter as—"

"This is entirely fictitious, in every way," he assured her. "So, I'll just sit here while you read it. No, wait. You wanted to go back to sleep, so—"

Jen groaned and hit him with her pillow. "When you get that hurt-puppy look on your face you are truly pathetic, Dawson. Allow me to make a pot of coffee first—"

Knock knock knock at her door.

"Jennifer?" her grandmother called out. "Are you up?"

Jen put her finger to her mouth, indicating that Dawson should be quiet. He had climbed in through her window, using the ladder that normally led to *his* window. If her grandmother found out, she'd freak.

"Yeah, but I'm going back to sleep, Grams."

"I just want to come in for a moment to tell you—"

"No!" Jen warned, but it was too late. The door opened. Grams stood there, and practically quivered with disapproval at the sight of Jen, clad only in a skimpy T-shirt and panties, in bed with the boy from next door.

"Before you give birth over this, Grams," Jen began, "we were just talking about Dawson's new script. He brought it over." She held it up for her grandmother to see.

Grams ignored her and focused on Dawson. "How did you get into my house, young man?"

Dawson pointed at the window.

"Then you will kindly exit the same way you entered."

"All right," Dawson agreed, getting up. "We really were just talking, though."

It was Grams' turn to point at the window.

"Call me when you've read it," Dawson told Jen, easing himself outside. "Or come over. Use the ladder and—"

"Good-bye, Mr. Leery," Grams said, her voice mirthless.

"Good-bye," Dawson replied, and he disappeared.

Grams turned on Jen. "This is a Christian home, Jennifer. I will tolerate none of that behavior here."

"*What* behavior? Nothing was going on."

Her grandmother sat on the end of her bed. "I know we've had our problems, Jennifer, our disagreements about the right choices to make in life."

"Grams, please, it's way too early for this—"

"And I know how much you miss your grandfather," her grandmother continued. "But our relationship has improved, don't you think?"

Jen nodded warily. She really did love Grams. And their relationship *had* improved. But sometimes it was like they were speaking different languages without a translator.

"I want you to think about this, Jennifer," Grams said. "Just because you did certain things that you regret back when you lived in New York, doesn't mean you have to continue that behavior here in Capeside."

"Look, Grams, I don't want to offend you, but you've played this song for me before."

"But it's apparent that you've neglected to learn the lyrics," her grandmother said archly.

"Grams, Dawson and I are friends. Period. And my personal life is personal. You're just going to have to accept that."

"Well, if I can't influence your behavior, perhaps Courtney will," her grandmother said primly.

Jen shook her head. "Courtney? As in Cousin-from-Hell Courtney?"

"Why must you belittle your cousin? It's ugly."

"And why do you still buy her Courtney the Perfect act?" Jen retorted, stung.

"It's sad when family turns on family," Grams said. "I hope this visit will change things for the two of you."

"I still don't know why she's coming," Jen declared. "The last time I saw her wasn't exactly a *Touched by an Angel* moment. Dawson and Pacey crashed her sweet sixteen, and Joey punched one of her friends."

"I know what happened," Grams said dryly. "And her version of what occurred is slightly different from yours. The Fields boy's nose was broken, you know."

Jen smirked at the memory. "He deserved it. Knowing that Joey did that is almost enough to make me love her. When's Courtney's impending visit happening, anyway?"

"This afternoon."

"*What?*" Jen yelped.

"Really, Jennifer, save the histrionics. Courtney's parents went to their beach house in the Hamptons, and at the last minute Courtney decided not to go with them and to come today instead of next weekend. Isn't that lovely?"

"No," Jen snapped. "Do I have any say in this?"

"No," Grams replied, as sweet as her granddaughter was sour. "She's arriving around three. I'm sure you'll want to be here to greet her."

Then, ignoring Jen's scowls, Grams got up and

handed her Dawson's script. "Here, dear. Plenty of time to read Mr. Leery's latest opus before your cousin arrives."

"You realize this visit is going to be a disaster, don't you?" Jen asked.

"What you need is a more positive attitude, Jennifer," Grams said briskly, as she headed for the door. "Courtney has always had a very positive attitude. You'd do well to let some of that rub off on you while she's here."

Grams shut the door behind her. She didn't see the script to *Don and Dulcie* fly across the room, a victim of Jen's frustration.

"It's really exciting, Pacey," Andie said as she led Pacey into the living room. "I mean, can you believe I'm a Capeside Romance Festival convert?"

Andie had just come from the first meeting of the hosts and hostesses of the Capeside Romance Festival. She'd applied because her financial situation was just south of desperate these days, and she'd heard that the money would be excellent. With her father pulling his disappearing act, and her mom having recurring mental problems, Andie's days of living the Rhode Island rich life seemed like something she'd dreamed, not something she'd experienced.

It hadn't been easy to move to Capeside, and her many family secrets hadn't stayed secret for very long. But she had her brother, Jack. And she had made some friends in Capeside. And there was Pacey.

Who would have thought that Andie McPhee, the

honor student who color-coordinated her study notes, would fall for the town clown?

But they were all so wrong about him. Pacey was . . . well, amazing. Funny. Smart. Loving. Sweet. Hot. The fact that his father, the town's beloved Chief of Police, had written off his younger son as a loser had caused Pacey to grow up believing it. But it wasn't true. And ever since Andie had come into his life, he had begun to prove his father wrong.

Pacey plopped down next to Andie on the living room couch and draped one arm around her. "So, what will you be doing for the festival?"

"Well, there are twenty of us hosts and hostesses," Andie explained, "and we all wear these cute 'Capeside *Is* Romance' T-shirts. Ours are red with white letters and the ones for sale to the public will be white with red letters. That's how people will know who we are."

"Diabolical," Pacey said, nodding.

"Basically, our job is to make sure all the tourists have a great time," Andie said. "You know, meet and greet, make special arrangements for VIPs—"

"What VIPs?"

Andie shrugged. "Got me. Oh, and we give guided tours on these little trolleys that have been rented for the weekend of the festival. You know, like at Disney World."

Pacey pretended to hold a microphone to his mouth. "Ladies and gentlemen, on your right is Screenplay, our generic video store. And on your left, our generic supermarket. Oh, and don't miss that stoplight. Pure romantic excitement—you never know when it will change."

Andie leaned back against his arm. "Come on, Pacey. Capeside really is beautiful. Down by the creek, the docks, the incredible sunsets. After all, we fell in love here."

"Good point." He leaned over to kiss her.

"Pacey, did you take my Ralph Lauren sweater?" an irritated voice boomed down the hall. Two seconds later, the owner of the voice, Pacey's older brother Doug, stood in the doorway. "Oh, hi, Andie. How goes it?"

"It goes fine, thanks," Andie said.

Doug glowered at his brother. "Well?"

"I know how overly important name-brand fashions are to men of your persuasion," Pacey said, "and I could weep with happiness that you found the means to purchase a Ralph Lauren sweater on your measly deputy cop salary, but, alas, I do not know where your sweater is."

Doug sighed a long-suffering sigh. "The sweater was a gift, Pacey. And I promised the very lovely *woman* who gave it to me that I would wear it *on our date.*"

Pacey turned to Andie, his hands clasped dramatically over his heart. "It's touching that Deputy Doug would date a woman just to please his loving family, don't you agree?"

Andie jabbed Pacey in the side with her elbow. "Come on, Pacey. You know Doug isn't gay."

"Thank you, Andie," Doug said with wounded gravity. "Sometime you'll have to explain to me what it is you see in my brother."

23

"A sense of humor?" Andie ventured.

Pacey snorted out a laugh.

Doug stabbed a finger at him. "If you have my sweater, Pacey, you will regret it." He turned on his heel and left.

"There's something about my brother—besides the uniform—that always makes me think of Hitler Youth," Pacey said with a shudder.

"Maybe I can help you stop thinking about it," Andie said. She leaned over and gave him the softest, sweetest of kisses. "How's that?"

"What brother?" Pacey asked, pulling her to him again. This time the kiss was sizzling. "You know, McPhee, you're so good at that, I bet you could win a kissing contest."

She bolted upright. "Oh no, you don't, Pacey."

"No, I don't what?"

She folded her arms. "You know very well what. You are not going to talk me into being in a public kissing contest just so you can drive a Viper for a week!"

"Okay, I'll forget talking you into it," Pacey agreed. "How about if I grovel-pathetically you into it?"

"You *are* pathetic, and how about if you take no for an answer?"

Pacey snapped his fingers. "Junk food. That's what you need. Junk food always weakens your resolve." He got up and pulled her up, too.

"There's nothing you can say or do that's going to get me to change my mind," she told him as they walked to the kitchen.

He got a box of chocolate chip cookies out of the

cupboard and poured her a glass of milk. "Why are you so dead set against this?"

Andie leaned on the counter and nibbled a cookie. "This is how I see it. Except for the very occasional, entirely spontaneous, you-just-can't-help-yourself public embrace, our kisses are a very private thing. Besides, I just don't need the pressure right now."

He put his arms around her waist. "I'm touched."

"And I'm eating." She reached around him for the bag of cookies.

"You could look at it as, say, a performance," Pacey suggested. "We could pretend to be other people. Hey, we could even enter dressed as famous lovers! Then they would be in the kissing contest, and not us."

She raised her eyebrows dubiously. "Do I look like I'm buying that one, Witter?"

"No," he admitted. "Cut me some slack, I'm thinking on my feet here."

She reached for another cookie. "You might as well give up, Pacey. I'm not going to change my mind."

Clad now in a beautiful blue sweater, Doug hurried into the kitchen and rummaged through some papers near the phone. "Where did I leave that address?"

"Is that the sweater that I allegedly purloined?" Pacey asked.

"I didn't accuse you, I asked you. Ah, here it is." Doug stuck the paper in his wallet. "Tell Dad I won't be here for dinner, okay?"

"Sure thing," Pacey agreed easily. "Oh, Doug, listen. Since your date won't be getting any studly action from you, could you ask her if she has any interest in entering the kissing contest with your very hetero sibling?"

"You're sick, Pacey," Doug said, and walked out.

"Thank you," Pacey said with pride.

Andie laughed. "I am so on to you."

"What?"

"That little remark was supposed to tick off your brother and, at the same time, get me to feel threatened so that I'll agree to be in the kissing contest with you."

Pacey wagged his finger at her. "You're way too smart for your own good, McPhee."

She took a big swallow of milk. "Way too smart for *your* good, you mean."

This time he succeeded in getting his arms around her waist. "Yeah," he admitted softly, tenderly touching her cheek. "Way too good for me, period."

"See, that's where you're wrong, Pacey." Her arms snaked around his neck. "Totally wrong. Now shut up and kiss me."

"You can't be serious," Joey said, putting down her sketch pad. She had been drawing at a picnic table behind the Ice House, on break during the after-lunch lull, when Jen had dropped the bomb on her: Jen was on her way back to Grams' house to meet Courtney, who was arriving for a visit.

"Totally serious," Jen said, sitting next to Joey. She tried to sneak a look at Joey's drawing, but Joey quickly shut the sketch pad. "Anyway, I figure forewarned is forearmed, something like that."

"But Courtney hates you, me, us," Joey said.

"Tell me about it," Jen agreed.

"The one and only time I met her was when I punched her idiot friend Danny. Not that he didn't deserve it for bragging to everyone that he supposedly had sex with me. How long is she staying?"

Jen pushed some hair off her forehead. "I plan to do my best to talk her into chowing down on the feast Grams is preparing even as we speak, and then getting out of here."

"Good luck," Joey said dubiously.

Jen hugged her knees to her chest. "So, not to change the subject, but did you know Dawson wrote a new film for that romance contest thing?"

"No," Joey replied, her tone turning frosty. "And I'm sure you're beyond thrilled that you *do* know. I suppose you'll be working on it with him in some intimate capacity, like you did with his last film. Have fun."

Jen peered at Joey. "You know, this balancing act you and I are doing really demeans us both. I thought we'd gotten beyond this."

Joey shrugged, clearly uncomfortable.

Jen looked out at the harbor. "Remember that day we spent talking with Dawson's mom? 'What Teen Girls Want,'" she said mockingly, referring to Gale's human-interest piece for the local news. "What a riot."

"Yeah, I loved speaking for millions of teen girls," Joey said sarcastically. "Most of the time I can barely speak for myself."

"It's not the group therapy portion of the proceedings that stayed with me," Jen explained. "It was something you said to me afterwards. That you respect me. Remember?"

Joey nodded.

"That meant something to me, Joey. Because I respect you, too. There have been moments in the past when we've even been friends. And we can both be friends with Dawson."

Joey gave her a tight smile. "You might still think of me as that utterly naive, impossibly tall girl who has barely been outside of Capeside, but that's not exactly who I am anymore. It's time you saw that."

Jen shielded her eyes from the sun with her hand. "Which means?"

"Which means we both know that in this case the word 'friend' is heavily loaded," Joey went on. "And I for one do not care which one of us happens to be 'friendlier' with Dawson on any given day."

"Right." Jen got up and started to walk away, then turned back to Joey. "You know, you're right. You're not as naive as you used to be, Joey. What you are now is a really, really bad liar."

Joey opened her mouth to protest.

"You care," Jen said before Joey could speak. "You care so much that you still find the need to lie about it." She slipped on her sunglasses.

"And for your information," she continued, "I *will* be working with Dawson on his film. Intimately. Yes, it's a love story. But this time, it's not about you."

Chapter 3

Jen leaned against a tree in Grams' front yard and watched for Courtney's car to pull into the driveway. Courtney had called for directions a few minutes before from a gas station in town. It meant that, in just moments, one of the people she loathed most in the world would be air-kissing the vicinity of her cheeks in that affected European way that Courtney had picked up from her mother.

Courtney would be wearing whatever the hot designer of the moment was showing in ridiculous, overpriced casual wear. Her hair would be perfect. Nails, ditto. The pearls around her neck and the diamond studs in her ears would not only be real, they'd be insured family heirlooms.

Oh, and the luggage in the trunk would be designer too, of course. Jen wouldn't have been surprised if Courtney had dragged one of her family's servants with her from New York just to unload her two dozen bags.

A pink Saab with a specially ordered pale pink leather interior pulled into the driveway. Courtney. Pale pink was Courtney's favorite color. Courtney waved gaily at Jen as the car rolled to a stop. Then she got out.

Jen was floored by how she looked. She was wearing cute denim overalls over a simple ribbed T-shirt, and ordinary sandals, with nary a designer label in sight. Her long blond hair was pulled back in a casually messy ponytail.

"Jen!" she threw herself into her cousin's arms. "I'm so glad to see you!"

Jen stood in a state of semi-shock. "Hi," she managed.

"This is so fantastic, isn't it?" Courtney went on, looking around. "It's going to be so much fun to hang out with you in Capeside."

Jen eyed her warily. "You didn't by any chance join some mind-twisting cult I don't know about, did you?"

Courtney giggled. "Of course not, silly!"

"Then why are you dressed like you live here instead of like the social-climbing New Yorker I know and loathe?"

Courtney stuck her lower lip out and pouted. "Now, Jen, is that nice?"

"I was going for honest, actually," Jen said. "When Grams told me you were coming to visit, surprise doesn't begin to cover my reaction. And now you're here, looking like *that*. Which leads me to think: What's up with you?"

"What is up with me?" Courtney echoed. "You mean why would I skip the Hamptons and come here instead?"

"Something along those lines, yeah."

Courtney leaned in confidentially. "I'll be honest with you, okay? I missed Grams. A lot. And I know you find this hard to believe, Jen, but I missed you, too."

"In what parallel universe?" Jen asked.

"Okay, I know we haven't always gotten along—"

"We've *never* gotten along," Jen said.

"Okay, we've never gotten along." Courtney shoved her hands into the deep pockets of her overalls. "You were always the ultracool, rebellious cousin and I was always the sweet, play-by-the-rules cousin. And you know what, Jen? Here's my deep, dark secret. I could never compete with you. I was always secretly jealous and I—"

"Hold it right there," Jen interrupted. "I seem to recall that sweet, play-by-the-rules Courtney stabbed me in the back at every opportunity. The entire family has thrown you in my face forever. 'Courtney is so well bred and well groomed and sweet and considerate and *virtuous*,'" she said, imitating the adults in their family. "'*And then there's Jen.*'"

The two girls stared at each other.

"Isn't there a nicer place than Grams' front yard where we could continue this discussion?" Courtney asked.

Jen thought for a moment. "Well, there are the docks. The view's good, if you like fishing boats."

"I love fishing boats. Let's go," Courtney decided.

"I can unpack later. Want to drive the Pink Panther?"

Jen shook her head. Courtney asking if she wanted to drive? Something was definitely up. The question was, what?

Fifteen minutes later, the two of them were sitting on a bench overlooking the docks, watching the fishing boats putter out at no-wake speed. It was a peaceful scene, but Jen was still feeling extremely wary.

"They all bought the act, Courtney," Jen told her, her eyes cold. "Hell, they still buy it. Don't be surprised if Grams fixes you up a nice stable to sleep in, because I'm pretty sure she thinks you're the Virgin Mary. You run a great game, Courtney. But you can't run it on me."

"I know," Courtney said softly. "You're right. I suck." She looked down and pensively twisted a metal button on her overalls. "I'm glad you called me on it, Jen."

"You are?"

Courtney nodded. "I'm tired of living a lie. I know I've been terrible to you. I really want to change that."

Jen folded her arms. "Why?" she asked cynically.

Courtney shrugged. "Because you're my first cousin. And maybe because I'm finally growing up a little. Look, I don't expect you to just believe me. I know I'll have to prove it to you. And I'm ready to do that. If you'll give me the chance."

Jen eyed her skeptically, pushing some hair off

her forehead. "If you're running another game on me, Courtney, I swear I will make you sorry."

"Think about it, Jen. What possible ulterior motive could I have?"

"That's what I'm trying to figure out," Jen grumbled.

Courtney grinned at her cousin. "Come on, Jen, look at what I'm wearing! I wanted to fit in, so I bought a whole bunch of clothes at The Gap. I look like every high school girl from . . . from Long Island or something. Now, that proves I'm serious, doesn't it?"

Jen had to laugh. "I have to admit, knowing that nothing you're wearing ever sashayed down a runway on a supermodel does add some weight to your argument."

"Exactly," Courtney agreed. Her huge, startlingly blue eyes looked into Jen's. "Maybe we can start all over with each other, Cuz. Do you think we can try, at least?"

"What I think is that—"

"Hey, it's Jen, isn't it?" a sexy male voice asked from behind them.

Jen turned around. The gorgeous Ryan Phillippe look-alike she'd met at the Ice House was standing there, just as gorgeous as he had been before.

"Yeah, it is. Drake, right?" Jen smiled at him. "What are you doing here?"

"A friend's arriving by boat from Nantucket," he explained. "I'm just waiting for him."

"No, I meant, what are you still doing in town? I ran into you like a while back," Jen said. "Aren't

33

you just a spend-a-day-in-Capeside-and-try-to-get-lucky tourist?"

Drake laughed. "Not exactly. I'm staying here with my cousins for a month."

Jen's smile grew even wider. "Nice," she said flirtatiously. "Oh, speaking of cousins, this is my cousin—"

"Courtney," Courtney filled in, gracefully insinuating herself between Jen and the guy. "And I already know your name. Drake Keller."

"How very Amazing Kreskin of you," Jen said. "Are you having a Psychic Friends moment?"

"Don't you know who he is?" Courtney asked Jen, her eyes not wavering an instant from Drake.

"Yeah, he's a guy with dubious taste in friends-of-friends I met at the Ice House," Jen said.

"Don't you ever watch soaps? *Beacon Bay?*" Courtney asked. "Drake was on that show for three months last winter. He played Nick, Mariah's rebel boyfriend from the poor side of town."

"I was hoping they'd make me a regular," Drake said. "But they killed me off in a bus plunge when the show changed exec producers."

"I was so mad," Courtney told him fervently. "I taped that show every day because of you, and when that bus went over the cliff in the ice storm I quit watching. I should write them a protest letter!"

"That'd be great," Drake said. "On soaps they never hesitate to bring you back from the dead."

Jen turned to him. "And here I thought you were just some reasonably cute college student staying in our tacky little seaside community for one evening."

" 'College student' is flattering," Drake said. "But

the truth is, I'll be a senior in high school in the fall."

"Wow, that is so incredible," Courtney said, standing up and moving close to Drake. Jen stood, too.

Drake shrugged. "It's no biggie. I live in L.A. Believe me, where I live half the kids my age have acting résumés that put mine to shame."

"I'd love to hear more about it," Courtney purred.

"Well, I—oh, the launch from Nantucket's pulling in. Uh, anyone have a piece of paper?"

Jen fished in her pocket for a Capeside Romance Festival flyer that someone had thrust at her as she and Courtney had walked to the docks. "How's this?"

"A start," Drake said. "But no pen."

"How's this?" Courtney pulled a pink lip pencil out of the pocket of her overalls.

Drake wrote a phone number on the paper, then handed the paper to Jen and the lip pencil to Courtney. "I hope I didn't wreck your lip stuff," he told her.

"Don't give it a thought," Courtney assured him. "You know, I just arrived from New York to visit Jen. I don't know my way around Capeside at all, Drake. Maybe we can explore it together."

"Yeah, maybe," he said. "So, talk to you soon, ladies." He hurried down to where the launch was tying up.

"Oh, my God, I can't believe Drake Keller is in Capeside!" Courtney squealed.

"Big deal, Courtney, he's just some guy from a soap."

"I'm telling you, he's going to be the next Leonardo and Brad rolled into one," Courtney said. "You heard it here first." She shielded her eyes from the sun and looked at Drake on the dock. "Drake and I might be soul mates, don't you think?"

"I think we'd better get to Grams' and unload your stuff now," was Jen's only reply.

"Okay!" Courtney said brightly. "Are you sure you don't want to drive?"

Jen didn't reply, so Courtney led the way back to her car, slid into the driver's seat, and followed Jen's terse directions to Grams' house.

"I am so psyched," Courtney went on as she took a curve too fast along the beach road. "Drake and I are meant to be."

Jen felt her irritation rising. "You don't even know him! And I thought you and Billy were 'meant to be.'" Billy was Jen's ex. She'd heard that he and Courtney were seeing each other. And even though she didn't want Billy back, it still irked her.

"Oh, that." Courtney flashed a quick smile, then looked back at the road. "It's kind of over. So listen, we'll call Drake later, okay? And see if he wants to hang out? Are there any hot parties we can invite him to?"

"Gee, you sound just like these thirteen-year-olds I met the other night," Jen said wryly. "Anyway, you're on your own with soap-stud tonight. I'll be with Dawson, working on the script for his new film."

"Dawson?" Courtney grimaced. "Isn't he that guy with the blond hair who crashed my Sweet Sixteen and—"

"That's Dawson," Jen said. "And I'm warning you, Courtney. Be cool with my friends while you're here. Take the next right."

She did. "I will be, I promise," Courtney said. "I'm sure that I don't know the real Dawson or Joelle or— What was that other guy's name?"

"Pacey," Jen filled in. "And it's not Joelle. It's Joey."

"What unique names," Courtney said sweetly. "Anyway, I'm sure I got the wrong impression of them and they got the wrong impression of me. Let's all be like little kids and call 'do-over.' How's that?" She glanced quickly at Jen.

Jen didn't reply. As far as she was concerned, the jury was still out on Courtney. But the verdict was leaning toward a big, fat "guilty."

"Bessie, do you mind if I cut out early?" Joey asked her sister as she added up Deputy Doug's check and put it under his coffee cup at the counter.

"Thanks, Joey," Doug said, finishing his coffee.

"No prob," Joey told him. She turned to her sister, who was refilling the silverware tray. "Well?"

Bessie checked her watch. "Let's see, it's six o'clock, but it's pretty dead in here tonight. I'll make you a deal. I'll handle dinner tonight if you handle breakfast in the morning. I need to take Alexander to the clinic for a checkup."

"Deal," Joey agreed, taking off her apron. She kissed her sister on the cheek, grabbed her backpack, and headed out the door. She rode her bicycle to Dawson's house. Her heart beat faster, which was ridiculous. So what if she hadn't told him she was coming over? She never used to tell him ahead of time, so why should it be any different now?

Because everything is different now, Joey told herself. You're only going over there because Jen told you about Dawson's new movie. Which is more than Dawson told you.

She knocked lightly on the screen door when she got there. "Anyone home?" she called through the screen.

The interior door was open, to let in the cool New England night air. No one answered. Gale's car was gone. But that didn't mean Dawson wasn't home. He never could hear the front door if he was watching a video in his room.

"Hello?" she called again. No answer. She went inside and took the stairs two at a time up to Dawson's room.

It was empty. She lay down on his neatly made bed and thought about all the hours over the years that she'd spent with Dawson in that bedroom and on that bed. How she'd hidden out there when her mom got so sick. How she'd slept in his bed with him, his arm around her, and found a safety that didn't exist in her rundown home across the creek.

It had been so innocent back then.

It could never be that innocent again.

It wasn't that Joey wanted them to be a couple again, because she didn't. Not now. But the feelings in her heart were real. They didn't go away just because she was trying to figure out who she was and what she needed apart from Dawson Leery.

Joey wandered over to his closet and pulled out

his favorite flannel shirt. She held it to her nose, inhaling deeply. It smelled just like Dawson.

"Joey?"

She whirled around. It was Dawson, with a rolled-up script in his hands.

"Hi!" She was red-faced, his shirt still in her hands. "I was . . . uh . . ." She looked at his shirt. "Thinking about *The Miracle Worker!* Did you ever wonder how intensely developed Helen Keller's sense of smell must have been?"

"Not recently," Dawson replied, sitting on the end of his bed.

"Oh. Well, it was just on Nick at Nite," Joey ad-libbed while hanging Dawson's shirt back in the closet. "So it got me thinking. Patty Duke was amazing as a child actor."

"Did you come over to talk about Hollywood talent who peaked in prepuberty?" Dawson asked. "Not that I'm complaining, Joey, because I'm not. Finding you in my room is the most pleasant of surprises."

"Always happy to contribute to the sunshine of your day, Dawson," Joey said, leaning against the wall. "So, speaking of movies. I heard you wrote a script for the 'Capeside *Is* Romance' contest. A love story."

"That was not the smoothest of transitions."

"Kindly do not rewrite me, Dawson," Joey said. "I was merely expressing a friendly interest in your latest artistic endeavor."

"Thanks."

Joey cocked her head at him. "That's it? 'Thanks'? No self-obsessed monologue about the minutiae of your latest opus of passion? No explanation, no defensive denial about what—or who—might have been the inspiration for it?"

Dawson smiled. "You want to know if it's about you."

"Incorrect." Joey sat next to him. "I care about your art, Dawson. I always have. I always will."

"That means a lot to me, Joey. But if you're willing to be 'the woman behind the man,' even if it is in the capacity of friend as opposed to . . . whatever, then why won't you let me be 'the man behind the woman'?"

She looked at him blankly.

"In other words, Joey, if you want to read my script, let me see your artwork. I've hardly seen any of your sketches—and let's not forget how I ended up seeing your sketch of Jack!"

She nervously puffed some air out from between her lips. "You know what I always say, Dawson. Behind every great woman is a great behind."

"Amusing," Dawson commented, "but you digress."

"Right." Joey sat there for a few moments.

"Okay, fine," she said, getting up to retrieve her sketch pad from her backpack. "You can see the stupid drawing I was doing. But you have to realize, Dawson, that while you've been film-obsessed since you first saw *E.T.*—art is a fairly new endeavor for me."

"Do you think I somehow wouldn't be supportive of you, Joey? Don't you know me better than that?"

"What I'm hoping is that you won't be patronizing." She sat next to him again, and opened her sketch pad to the sketch she'd been working on that afternoon. "It's not done yet," she added hastily.

"This is excellent, Joey. Really."

She stared at it, frowning. "No. It's not. It's a start. I feel so frustrated sometimes, seeing exactly what I want in my mind and not being able to get it on paper."

He looked at her. "That's exactly how I feel when I try to get the right words on paper."

He was so close. She could smell his wonderful, clean, Dawson smell. It was scary to her, how much power he had over her feelings, how much she still wanted *him*.

Still wanted to kiss him.

He moved closer. "Joey," he whispered.

She forced herself to jump up and put her sketch pad away so that he couldn't kiss her. Because everything was just too confusing. If she wasn't ready to commit to him, then she couldn't very well start rolling around with him on his bed. And she felt pretty certain that for them there wasn't very much space between one kiss and rolling around.

"Okay," she said brightly. "So fair's fair. Do I get to read your script now?"

Dawson sighed. "Don't you think we should talk about what just almost happened?"

"How about if we just almost talk about it?"

Dawson nodded. "Consider the subject changed, although I want to state for the record that we can return to this conversation at a later date."

"Counsel's objection is duly noted," Joey said dryly.

"Well, I'm calling the film *Don and Dulcie*. Basically, it's a modern teen Don Quixote searching for his Dulcinea in Capeside." He tossed Joey the script. "I see her as a girl who has been through a lot—family problems, money problems, guys who swore they loved her but were only using her.

"She feels scarred by it," Dawson continued, "and doesn't believe in love anymore. But Don falls in love with her—true love that will last for eternity. It's the purity of that eternal love that finally allows her to believe in love again."

"So basically it's a fairy tale," Joey said, eyeing the script so she wouldn't have to eye Dawson.

"Not at all," Dawson said quietly.

"Improvising a scene?" a sharp voice at the door asked.

Joey stepped quickly away from Dawson. "Hi, Jen."

"Hi," Dawson said.

"We had a script conference scheduled, right?" Jen asked in her best all-business voice.

"Right," Dawson agreed.

"Oh, I was just leaving," Joey said, quickly gathering up her stuff. She held the script out to Dawson. "Did you need this?"

"I have other copies," he assured her. "Take it."

Joey looped her backpack over one arm. She felt as self-conscious as if Jen had caught her naked with Dawson instead of just talking to him.

Jen sat on Dawson's bed and took out her own well-marked copy of the script, ignoring Joey.

Joey felt monumentally awkward. "So, Jen, did your cousin arrive okay?"

"Courtney the Perfect is next door even as we speak," Jen said, not looking at Joey.

"Wait, your cousin Courtney is here and no one told me?" Dawson asked incredulously. "The one who wanted to arrest us for what we did at her sweet sixteen party?"

"That would be her," Jen agreed. "She claims she's over it. Anyway, right now she's hyperventilating over the fact that she has a date tonight with this guy, Drake Keller, who was on—"

"*Beacon Bay*," Dawson filled in. "I met him yesterday. The aunt he's visiting is a friend of my mom's. He's going to do the male lead in *Don and Dulcie*. He liked the time capsule idea. But how does Courtney know him?"

"Actually, I met him at the Ice House and then we ran into him this afternoon. And thanks for casting him without even discussing it with your producer, Dawson."

"Sorry, Jen, but I went to meet him and it was kind of spontaneous. He read for me, and he really has talent. It was an opportunity I couldn't pass up."

"You do realize that once word gets out, every female in Capeside is going to want to play Dulcie opposite him, don't you, Dawson?" Joey asked.

"If you're right, then that's a good thing," Dawson said. "I don't need to remind you of the hell we went through trying to find a leading lady for *Creek Daze.*"

Joey looped her hair behind her ears. "Well, I haven't read this opus yet, so I don't know who

would be right for the part. Is Dulcie based on anyone, Dawson?"

"Which translates to 'Is she based on me?' " Jen
said.

"Not at all," Joey insisted. "It's a simple question.
For all I know, Dawson based his leading lady on
you, Jen."

Both girls stared at Dawson.

Dawson rubbed his chin, clearly uncomfortable.
"She isn't based on anybody. She's a romantic
archetype."

Joey frowned and risked a glance at Jen, who was
frowning too. Clearly neither girl was buying it.

"Been there, heard that," Jen sang out.

"Okay, I recognize that every character is, on a
certain level, drawn from what the writer has
known or experienced," Dawson admitted. "But I'm
telling you, Dulcie isn't either one of you."

Jen's lip curled into a small smile. " 'S funny,
Dawson. All we know about Dulcie in your script is
her horrible past. I mean, in the present she doesn't
appear to have a life. She's just this . . . this damsel
in distress, waiting to be redeemed by Don's love."

"That's not how I see her, really," Dawson said.
"But if that's how you see her, then it should be
patently obvious that she isn't based on either one
of you. I mean, the notion that either of you would
be this unformed, uncentered, deeply needy girl
who could be redeemed by love is laughable. Isn't
it?"

He looked from Joey to Jen and back to Joey.

The truly funny thing was, nobody was laughing.

Chapter 4

"**Y**eah, you sure know how to throw a party, Dawson," Pacey said sarcastically as he took another swig of Jolt cola and looked across Dawson's backyard at the gaggle of girls surrounding Drake. "That is, if you intended this to be a party for soap-stud over there."

It was two days later. Dawson and Jen had come up with the idea of combining the auditions for the role of Dulcie with a party in Dawson's backyard. Word had spread like wildfire that a hot soap actor was doing the male lead. So girls had, as predicted, come out of the woodwork for a chance to get cast as the love of his life.

Already twenty-three girls had read with Drake, and none of them had anything approaching talent. It was like a repeat of the nightmare of the *Creek Daze* auditions.

"The party-slash-audition concept seemed great in theory," Dawson said, sighing.

"Well, it should have remained theoretical," Pacey said. "Even my way-too-intelligent-to-fall-for-it girlfriend is over there, drooling on Drake."

Dawson looked across the yard again, and sure enough, there was Andie, held spellbound by whatever Drake was saying. At least Joey wasn't with Drake, but that might only have been because Bessie had a killer migraine headache, and Joey had to cover for her at the Ice House. Dawson felt that a party without Joey didn't really seem like a party at all.

"Hey, Dawson," Chris Wolfe said cheerfully, clapping Dawson on the back. "Your party sucks, man." Chris was in their class at school, and he'd been in Dawson's last film. A major player, he was basically a sleaze who scored way too often.

"No need to hold back on how you really feel," Pacey said expansively. "Let Dawson have it."

"Here's how I see it, Dawson," Chris said, sipping from a paper-bagged beer he had brought with him. "There are three couples dancing to the lame-ass boom box you set up, and other than that, just about every other babe is over there with soap-boy. Which leaves a whole lot of dudes wandering around by their lonesome with that horn-dog thing going on." He saluted Dawson with his beer.

"If I might remind you two, the main purpose of this party is to audition for the role of Dulcie," Dawson said.

Across the yard, Andie laughed aloud at something Drake had said.

Pacey groaned. "Can you please explain to me why Andie McPhee, a woman of such obvious intelligence and beauty, would be willing to publicly drool over some guy who was once on a soap, but be unwilling to enter a public kissing contest with me?"

"You know, Pacey, everyone wants to be near the famous," Jen said as she wandered over. She checked the list of names on her clipboard. "Bad news, Dawson. Every girl who signed up to audition has already auditioned. Badly."

"What about Dina?" Chris joked.

Jen looked over at Chris' little sister. "I crossed her off the list since she has yet to shake hands with puberty."

Dawson's eyes slid over to Dina, who was sitting alone, stuffing potato chips in her mouth. Dina had once tried to blackmail him into kissing her, which had shocked him. She was just a little kid! Everything changes, no matter what you want, Dawson thought. I wish I could tell Dina to enjoy being a kid while she still can, and—

"Yo, Dawson!" Pacey called, waving a hand in front of his face.

Dawson blinked. "Sorry, what?"

"*What* is that we don't have our Dulcie," Jen reminded him.

"We could ask Courtney to audition," Dawson suggested wryly. "You said she went out with the guy. Maybe they'd have chemistry, at least."

Jen shrugged. "When I left, she was getting dressed. Why she hasn't made the big trek from next door is a mystery to me. But trust me, you don't want her."

"I know that, Jen," Dawson said. "And since I haven't seen her since she allegedly arrived in Capeside sort of illustrates that she doesn't want anything to do with me."

Pacey wagged a finger at Jen. " 'Fess up, Jen. You've got Courtney roped and gagged in your closet, right?"

"Sounds interesting," Chris said. "Is your cousin as hot for it as you are, Jen?"

"Ooo, nasty," Pacey commented.

Dawson felt his hands clenching into fists. He felt like smashing one into Chris' face but restrained himself.

Jen tapped one finger against her lips and considered. "You know, now that I think about it, Chris, you and Courtney deserve each other. No pesky ethics or morals to get in the way of a good time. I'll be sure to introduce you."

"Cool, I'll be around," Chris said smugly. He wandered off.

"And I thought you fumigated your backyard," Pacey said, as Chris departed. "Yet there goes walking vermin."

"Look, forget Chris," Jen said. "We need a Dulcie. And the only logical choice we have left is me."

"You can't produce *and* star in the film, Jen," Dawson told her.

"It's called being a 'hyphenate,' Dawson, and it happens in Hollywood all the time."

"Hyphenate. I like that," Pacey said. "Excuse me, you two, but I think I'll go present the notion to Andie that she can be a soap-stud groupie *and* kissing-contest winner hyphenate. Later."

Jen gave Dawson an ironic look. "I do have some experience as a girl who has been used by guys. And though I am loath to admit it, I do still believe in love."

Love. Did he love her? Did she love him? Or was it all just lust for both of them? He knew he liked her. A lot. And there had been a time when . . .

Stop it, Dawson, he told himself. This is no time to go off on that tangent.

"It's not that you can't play it, Jen," Dawson said. "It's that I need you to—"

"Hi," Courtney said brightly, coming up to them. "I'm so sorry I'm late for your party, Dawson. I got tied up on a call to New York. Nice to see you again."

Dawson's jaw fell open. This Courtney looked nothing like the designer-clad, overproduced girl he'd met in New York. This Courtney was wearing a very simple long, pale pink cotton dress, no makeup, and her hair was held back by two scrunchies on either side of her head. She looked fresh, natural. Beautiful.

And where were the whining and the self-involved hysterics?

"Hi," Dawson managed. "Thanks for coming over."

"Thanks for inviting me," Courtney replied sweetly. "I've really been looking forward to seeing you and your friends again. I'm afraid we got off on the wrong foot in New York."

"It was our fault," Dawson insisted. "Pacey and I had no business crashing your party."

"Well, all the same, I apologize for being so rude that evening," Courtney said earnestly. "I think I was just so nervous because I wanted my sweet sixteen to be perfect that I overreacted." She held out her hand. "Truce?"

Dawson took it. "Truce." They shook.

"I hate to cut short this bizarre love fest," Jen said, "but we have to figure out what we're going to do, Dawson."

"Do about what?" Courtney asked.

"The female lead in Dawson's film," Jen said. "And don't even think about auditioning, Courtney. Because I'd sooner stick Pacey in drag and call him Tootsie than cast you."

Courtney flushed red with embarrassment.

"That's a little harsh, isn't it?" Dawson asked Jen.

"Not nearly harsh enough," Jen replied.

"It's okay, I wasn't going to audition," Courtney said easily. "Since I'm seeing Drake it probably wouldn't be a good idea for me to work with him. It could be messy."

"Whatever," Jen said dismissively. "Well, Dawson, either we bag this and set up another audition—which we don't have time to do—or you let me read with Drake."

"Or you let *me* read with Drake," another voice said.

Joey.

Dawson grinned. It was funny how just seeing her filled him with this helium-balloon happiness. Especially when seeing her was unexpected.

"Hey, Joey, I thought you were at the Ice House," Dawson said.

"Jack came in, and Bessie felt better and showed up. Actually, I think it's because a friend came to stay with Alexander and she was desperate for a baby reprieve." Joey's eyes slid over to Courtney.

"Hi," she said tentatively. "Uh, remember me?"

"Joelle," Courtney said, smiling.

"Joey," she corrected. "You seem . . . I don't know . . . different."

Courtney laughed. "I was just telling Dawson that I was afraid we had all gotten the wrong impression of each other in New York."

"Right, wrong impression," Joey agreed tentatively.

"Wrong, right impression," Jen corrected.

Courtney hit Jen playfully on the shoulder. "Oh, you're such a tease, Cuz. Anyway, I'm really looking forward to getting to know all of you while I'm here."

"Cool," Joey said, but the look in her eyes didn't quite agree with the word from her mouth.

Across the yard, the group of girls parted like the Red Sea as Drake said good-bye and walked toward Dawson.

"Oh, hi, Courtney," he said easily when he saw her.

She kissed him on the cheek. "Long time no see."

"So, Dawson," Drake said, "you have anyone else to audition?"

"I'm afraid not," Dawson said. "I mean, not yet."

"What about me?" Jen and Joey said at the same time. Then they looked at each other.

"Jen, I told you, I really don't want you to be in the film and produce it," Dawson said. "And Joey, I know you're only joking."

"Why would I be joking?" Joey asked.

Dawson hesitated. "Because I once had to beg you to appear in my admittedly excruciatingly amateurish early efforts at filmmaking. You hated it."

"Well, your technique has improved considerably since then, Dawson," Joey said lightly. "We change, we grow. We audition."

Drake cocked his head at her. "I know you from somewhere, don't I?"

"See if this rings a bell," Joey said. " 'Do you want fries with that?' "

"Her sister owns the Ice House," Jen filled in. "She waited on you there."

"Oh, right!" Drake snapped his fingers. "Great burgers."

"Thanks, I'll tell my sister you said so," Joey said. She held out her hand. "I'm Joey Potter."

"Drake Keller." They shook, as Dawson looked from Joey to Drake and back to Joey.

He didn't like the way things were going. Not at all. For one thing, the audition scene ended in a kiss. For another . . . well, that one was enough.

Joey looked at Dawson. "I'm ready for my close-up, Mr. DeMille," she joked.

"Come on, Joey," Dawson began. "I know you're not serious."

"You see, Dawson, one of your many problems is that you think you know me far better than you actually know me," Joey remarked. "Because it just so happens that I'm entirely serious."

"Good," Drake said, grinning. "Do you have the audition scene?"

"Got it," Joey said, holding up the pages. "Where do you want us, Dawson?"

"I really do not think this is a good idea—"

"Dawson, could I speak to you a minute?" Jen asked, pulling him away from the others.

"What?" Dawson asked her, looking back over at Joey, who was laughing with Drake.

"Try to focus, Dawson," Jen said dryly. "Go ahead and let Joey audition. There's no chance she'll get the part. From what I've seen of Joey's past attempts at acting in your films, she has zero talent. Besides, if you stop her, you'll look like an idiot."

"Fine," Dawson said tersely. He marched back over to Joey and Drake. "Jen and I will audition you now."

"Hey, if she can audition, why can't I audition?" Dina pouted as a crowd began to form around them.

"Because the last time I checked, you were still whatever tender age it is that you are," Dawson replied.

"Age is meaningless, Dawson," Dina said coquettishly, giving him a sultry look.

Courtney giggled. "You are such a cutie!"

"Tell *him* that," Dina replied, folding her arms.

"Hey, chill out, kid," Pacey told her, putting his arm around Dina's slender shoulders. "Tell you what. The next time Dawson writes a role for a little kid, I will personally insist that he consider you for the role."

In reply, Dina stepped on Pacey's foot. Hard.

"Okay, everybody, if we could have quiet," Jen called, as Pacey yelped in pain. "Somebody turn off that CD!"

The music stopped, and everyone gathered round.

"All right," Dawson said. "I'm looking for a natural quality. Keep it simple. Don't try and act. Don't—"

"Can we just do it, please?" Joey broke in.

"Fine," Dawson snapped, stepping back. "Do it."

"Okay, take it from the top, please," Jen said.

Drake and Joey both looked down at their scripts. Joey waited a moment, then looked up. She was Dulcie now, not Joey.

"I don't understand what you want from me, Don."

"Nothing," Drake/Don said quietly, his eyes searching hers.

Joey/Dulcie laughed sardonically. "In my experience, everyone wants something."

"To look at you," Drake/Don said reverently. "To make you happy."

The scene went on, and the backyard was silent except for Drake's and Joey's voices. And then they were finished, but before Dawson could call "cut," Drake had taken Joey into his arms.

He kissed her. Gently, passionately, thoroughly.

Every girl watching sighed.

"Cut!" Dawson yelled. "The end!"

Drake and Joey broke apart self-consciously.

"Talk about chemistry," Andie mumbled loud enough for Dawson to hear.

"Did you want to give us notes or anything?" Drake asked Dawson.

"No, I saw more than enough," Dawson replied, an edge to his voice.

Someone turned the music back on, and a bunch of people began to dance wildly, as if watching Drake and Joey had heated everyone up. Dawson walked around to the front porch so he could cool off. Watching Joey kissing Drake Keller had not been his favorite experience in life.

"There you are," Jen said, stepping up onto the porch. "I've been looking for you. Playing the brooding artist, Dawson?"

He didn't speak as Jen sat down next to him.

"You know Joey was by far the best person we saw."

"She didn't have exactly the quality I'm looking for," Dawson insisted.

"Right," Jen muttered. "And that quality would be—?"

"It's difficult to put into words."

Jen looked up at the stars. "Admit it, Dawson. It made you crazy to watch Joey kissing Drake. If you don't cast her, that's the only reason why not."

"I really think you're underestimating my ability to separate my personal and professional lives, Jen."

"Uh-huh." She stood up and pulled him up, too. "Sleep on it, Dawson. We'll powwow tomorrow. Time to go back to the so-called party."

They went back around the house. A slow ballad was playing. The first thing Dawson saw was Joey. And Drake. Slow dancing. Very, *very* slow dancing.

"It's not sex, Dawson," Jen pointed out.

"It's close."

"They're upright and fully clothed. Dawson?"

His face was set in granite.

"Fine, catch you later when you regain the ability to speak," Jen said, walking off.

Dawson could barely breathe. Why was Joey dancing so close to Drake? She didn't even like to dance! Why was she gazing at him like that? Why was she—

"Dawson?"

It was Courtney.

"It's beautiful out, isn't it?" she asked him.

"Not in my experience, no," Dawson replied, his eyes still on Joey and Drake. If Courtney noticed his lack of attention, she didn't let on.

"Jen showed me your script for *Don and Dulcie*," Courtney said. "Paralleling the pure beauty of Capeside with the pure beauty of Don's love for Dulcie is really beautiful. It reminds me of the '57 Russian version of the Cervantes novel—so visually lavish and everything."

Now, Dawson turned to her. "Wait. Are you telling me that you actually *know* that film?"

"I took a foreign films course at the New School," Courtney explained. "It was fascinating. I can never look at a movie in exactly the same way anymore."

The music segued smoothly into another slow song.

"Would you like to dance?" Courtney asked Dawson.

Joey was still in Drake's arms, swaying blissfully to the music, looking way too happy.

"Sure," Dawson said. He took Courtney's hand and led her near where Joey and Drake were dancing, then he took her in his arms. As soon as he was sure Joey had noticed, he pulled Courtney even closer.

And then he realized what an idiot he was being. He pulled away from her slightly. "Sorry," he told her.

"For what?" She stared up at him, her lips slightly parted, her long eyelashes framing twin pools of blue.

"Just that I was completely out of line to hold you so close to me just now," Dawson explained.

She smiled up at him. "Do you know what word comes to mind when I look at you, Dawson? Chivalrous. Not unlike Don. Or Don Quixote. There are very few knights in shining armor around anymore, you know."

Dawson tore his eyes away from Joey. "It's extremely nice of you to say that, Courtney. I don't deserve it."

"Well, I think you do." She rested her cheek against his shoulder. He could smell her perfume, like June roses. "I guess you could just say I'm a romantic, old-fashioned girl," she sighed. "Believe me, I know how utterly out of style that is."

To Dawson's great surprise, he was starting to truly enjoy the silky feel of Courtney in his arms. "I think jaded has been done to death, actually," he told her.

"Me, too." Her eyes sparkled. "And everyone in New York is so jaded. I mean, if I ever admitted to my friends that I watch my favorite movie, *E.T.*, like once a week, all by myself, they would—"

"Wait. *E.T.* is your favorite movie?" Dawson asked.

Courtney looked flustered. "You aren't going to rag on me for it, too, are you?"

"Doubtful. It's my favorite, too," Dawson told her with a laugh. "True confession. I used to have my bedroom decorated in *E.T.*"

Courtney moved even closer into his embrace. "I just knew we misjudged each other back in New York, Dawson." She snuggled against him with a contented sigh.

"I think I'm beginning to agree with you," Dawson said. And to his own shock, he meant it. For the moment, Dawson Leery wasn't worrying about Joey and Drake at all.

Chapter 5

"**Y**ou're sure you're up for this?" Pacey asked Andie as he shakily stood up on his in-line skates.

"Skating in the park was my idea, remember?" Andie got up from the park bench. "Last night at Dawson's party, you gallantly offered to do whatever I wanted to do today."

"I am nothing if not a man of my word." He looked down at his skates. "So, what comes next?"

Andie sighed. "You've never skated before, Pacey?"

"I believe there was that one experience when I was six. I fell and broke my wrist."

"I'll try not to make this one quite as traumatic. See, you just push off on your right leg, then your left. Like this." She skated down the park's bike path, then turned around and smoothly skated back to him.

"You've been holding out on me, McPhee," he chided. "You didn't list Queen of the Newly-Resuscitated-and-Renamed Roller Jam on your job application."

"I might have taken a few lessons," she admitted. Pacey slid his right leg forward and wobbled dangerously. "Come on, Pacey." She took his hands and skated backward as he slowly skated forward.

"I could close my eyes and pretend we're doing a remake of *Ice Castles*," Pacey joked. " 'Oh please, give me the will to skate again!' " he cried in a dramatic falsetto.

Andie laughed. "Better stick to skating."

She spun around and they began to skate side by side. "See? Aren't we having fun?"

"My concept of having fun with you involves cherry-flavored body oil."

"Broaden your horizons," she said dryly, as they picked up speed.

"I love this!" Andie cried happily, as they gracefully skated around two joggers going in the other direction.

"I pulled that off quite gracefully, if I do say so myself," Pacey decided. "Did you notice how I—"

"Watch out!"

Too late. Pacey didn't see the stray Frisbee on the path. He skated onto it and fell on his butt. Hard.

"Are you okay?" Andie knelt beside him. "What hurts?"

Two little kids whizzed by and jeered at Pacey. "Only my ego," he told Andie. She tried to help him up, but he insisted that he could do it himself.

"Are you sure you're okay?"

"I'm thinking lunch break," Pacey said. He sat down on the grass next to the bike path, unlaced his skates, and replaced them with some flip-flops that he'd stashed in his pocket. "Is there a hot dog with everything at the snack bar with your name on it?"

"Two. And a Coke," Andie said. "Thanks."

Pacey, happy to be off the stupid skates, hurried to the snack bar and bought their lunch, then rejoined Andie.

"Two possibly carcinogenic dogs barking, one possibly carcinogenic beverage of choice." He handed them to her.

Andie took a huge bite of her hot dog, chewed it, and swallowed as Pacey sat down. "Now, this is what I call cuisine. Thanks, Pacey. This is so sweet. I mean, I know in-line skating wasn't high on your to-do list."

"We aim to please." He took a bite of his burger and smiled at her tenderly. "Have I mentioned how beautiful you look right now, Miss McPhee?"

She grinned and shook her head.

Pacey cleared his throat. Then he began to recite:

"She walks in Beauty, like the night
    Of cloudless climes and starry skies;
And all that's best of dark and bright
    Meet in her aspect and her eyes:
Thus mellowed to that tender light
    Which Heaven to gaudy day denies."

Andie practically choked on the last of her hot dog. "You memorized 'She Walks in Beauty' by Lord Byron?" she asked incredulously.

"What can I say? That poem *is* you, Andie."

Tears came to Andie's eyes. "Oh, Pacey . . ."

He took her hands in his and gazed soulfully into her eyes. "It so perfectly captures how much I love to hold you. To kiss you. Over and over and over. And over."

She pulled away from him abruptly. "You . . . you brat!" she sputtered.

"Moi?" Pacey asked innocently.

"This skating thing, and the love sonnet, it's all to get me to enter the kissing contest with you. Admit it!"

"Come on, McPhee, what are a few public kisses between two people who—"

She pushed him, making him lose his balance. He fell heavily to the ground. "Ouch," he said.

"You deserve worse," Andie seethed.

Pacey pushed himself back up to a sitting position. "Okay. I'm busted."

"You're slime, that's what you are."

"That, too," Pacey agreed. "Although the sonnet really does remind me of you."

"Stuff a wiener in it, Witter."

"Colorfully put. Come on, Andie, won't you please reconsider? If we win, which we will, it may be as close as I'll ever get to owning a Viper in this lifetime."

Andie's eyes narrowed and she crossed her arms. "Let me put it to you this way, Pacey. Kiss this."

Pacey hesitated. "So, would that be a final 'kiss-this,' or is it a I-still-have-a-shot-at-changing-your-mind 'kiss-this'?"

"What do you think?"

Pacey sighed and turned his head up to the sun. "I think I would have really enjoyed driving that Viper."

"To cast Joey or not to cast Joey, that is the question," Dawson mused aloud as he continued to pace across his carpet, exactly as he had done for the past hour.

Jen had called him early that morning to ask what his decision was and to point out again that if he didn't cast Joey, it would only be because his personal feelings were impinging on his art.

So much for Jen's previous theory that Joey had no acting talent.

But how could he direct Joey in passionate scenes with another guy? He'd almost lost it watching them kiss once!

But he didn't have another actress who could play the part. And if he didn't start shooting ASAP, he wouldn't have a complete video to enter in the contest.

But if he *did* cast Joey, then—

"Dawson?"

He turned around. Courtney stood in the doorway of his bedroom, wearing baggy jeans and a pale pink T-shirt. "I hope you don't mind that I just came up," she said hesitantly. "The front door was open."

"It's always open. No. I don't mind. What's up?"

She smiled. "I was about to ask you the same thing."

"I'm trying to decide who to cast as Dulcie."

Courtney nodded. "I heard Jen talking with you about it on the phone this morning. I know what a difficult decision it is. Casting is crucial. When I did my second student film at NYU I had six callbacks before—"

"Wait. You've acted in films?"

"Didn't I mention that?" She came into his room and sat on his bed. "I've been in three, actually. Student films, you know. But one of them made it into a few festivals."

"So, why didn't you audition for Dulcie yesterday?"

"Well, I hope this doesn't sound hopelessly elitist or anything," she began, "but it's just that I take acting very seriously. And I couldn't see auditioning in that party atmosphere. I mean, I don't think I could have concentrated enough to even find my character." She shrugged.

"But you want to audition?" Dawson asked hopefully. She could be the answer to all his problems.

"Oh, I'd love to," Courtney breathed. "But if it's too late . . ."

"No, no, not at all," Dawson insisted. He hurried to the phone. "Let me call Drake and see if he's available to read with you."

But Drake's aunt reported that Drake was in Boston and wasn't coming home until late tomorrow. He'd be back to start filming the day after tomorrow.

"Maybe I can get someone else to read with you," Dawson mused as he hung up the phone. "I can call Chris. He's not high on the food chain, but he—"

Courtney put her hand on his to stop him. "Dawson, I have an idea. Why don't I read with you?"

"With me? But I can't. I mean, I can't direct and be in the scene with you at the same time."

She shrugged. "Woody Allen does it. And Kenneth Branagh. And—"

"You're right." He looked at her. She really was so pretty. Not that pretty mattered, he quickly amended in his mind. But he couldn't help noticing.

"We could just get into character, you know, be Don and Dulcie, and improvise a scene," she suggested.

"Improvise?" Dawson echoed nervously. He felt infinitely more comfortable behind the camera than he felt in front of it. "I don't know if—"

Courtney got up and strode across his room. Then she turned back to him dramatically. "I don't know what you want from me, Don."

She had become Dulcie. An extremely melodramatic Dulcie. Dawson was at a loss.

Courtney/Dulcie lifted one fist in the air. "As God is my witness, guys always want something from me!"

"That's a little too *Gone With the Wind*, Courtney—"

"*Dulcie,*" she corrected, walking slowly toward him. "Don't you understand, Don? In my experience, and I've had a lot, guys are all alike."

Dawson's eyes skidded this way and that around his room. There was no escape. She was standing right in front of him. "Uh . . . not . . . any more than girls are all alike," he invented, though he felt like an idiot.

She swiftly sat next to him again. "Really? So what kind of guy are you then, Don?"

"I'm . . . uh . . ."

"The kind who wants me?" she asked. "Like all the others? Or do I dare hope that you're different?"

"Different," Dawson managed. "But listen, Courtney—"

"*Dulcie.*" She laughed bitterly. "How typical. Calling me by another girl's name."

"No, I meant—"

"I know what you meant. The truth is, Don, I can't hide my true feelings for you another moment. Even if you hurt me like all the others."

"I—"

That was as much as Dawson could get out of his mouth. Courtney had leaned over and snaked her arms around his neck. Before Dawson knew it, they were locked in a passionate embrace. And he was doing as much kissing as she was.

Hot. Hotter than hot. His IQ began a serious meltdown.

Finally she pulled away, giving him a luminous smile. "Was I okay?"

Was she *okay?* Oh, she meant her *acting.*

Dawson cleared his throat. "A little over the top," he told her. "But we could work on that. And I want to apologize if I stepped over the boundaries of acting just now—"

She put her index finger over his lips. "It was too special to spoil with words, Dawson. Do I get the part?"

The tiny part of his brain that had not turned to molten ooze knew her portrayal of Dulcie had been horrendous.

But not more horrendous than casting Joey.

"You'd have to work really hard to tone down the—"

"Oh, thank you!" Courtney squealed, throwing her arms around his neck again. "Thank you, thank you, thank you!"

So. It would appear *Don and Dulcie* had a leading lady.

Chapter 6

Two mornings later, at the crack of dawn, Dawson and Jen had assembled their crew, extras, and cast of two down by the creek to begin shooting their film. Capeside had been overcome by Romance Festival fever, which let them assemble a large group of eager volunteer helpers.

Dawson and Jen, however, were barely on speaking terms.

Jen had been disgusted when Dawson informed her that he'd cast Courtney instead of Joey. He'd insisted that Courtney had given a very powerful audition. She'd replied how interesting it was that these "powerful auditions" always seemed to take place when his producer—namely her—wasn't around.

He'd accused her of wanting Joey to be in the movie in the hope that Joey would fall for Drake.

She'd accused him of hiding behind some weenie

psycho-babble so that he wouldn't have to examine his own motives.

It had gone downhill from there.

Since their fight, their conversations had been strictly business, and Jen planned to keep it that way.

"Listen up, people," Jen called to the group of twenty or so kids. "Before we begin shooting *Don and Dulcie,* I want to thank all of you who have agreed to help with the film or to work as extras."

Dawson shifted his gaze from his camera, where he'd been framing a shot. "Right. Thanks."

"You guys, this short feature is going to be the hit of the Capeside Romance Festival," Andie called through cupped hands. She and Pacey were on hand to help, too. "So let's have a hand for our stars, Drake and Courtney!"

She began to clap, nudging Pacey hard with his elbow so that he'd applaud too. Some others dutifully joined in.

"Thanks, Andie," Courtney said sweetly. "But I think we should be applauding all of you for volunteering to work without getting the glory you deserve. I know you're doing it for Capeside and for the festival. So I just wanted to say thanks for making me welcome here."

"I'll second that," Drake agreed.

Jen could have gagged on the spot. Instead, she shot Courtney a look of jaded disbelief. Courtney just smiled.

"Okay, if the love fest is over, we're shooting the scene where Don sees Dulcie for the very first time, crying by the creek," Jen said, checking her scene breakdown list. "Extras, cross when Andie gives the signal. Any questions? Good. Places, please. Stand by."

"Uh, Dawson?" Courtney sidled up to him. "I just want to know. How is Dulcie feeling at this point?"

"Sad. Empty. Scared," Dawson instructed. "There's beauty all around you but you don't see it. You've been hurt too often and are afraid there's no guy on earth who would accept your past and still love you. But the real you, who is intrinsically untouched, is still innocent."

"That is so beautiful," Courtney choked out, tears filling her eyes. "So, what's my motivation?"

"Your motivation is that we're losing the dawn light," Jen snapped. "Can we just do the scene?"

"Sorry," Courtney said meekly. She hurried back to her assigned spot on the bank of the creek.

"Don't you think you were a little hard on her?" Dawson asked Jen, checking his viewfinder.

"Think about it, Dawson. Who does she remind you of? How about a female Sebastian from *Cruel Intentions?* She's scamming you. And you are so obviously ready, willing, and, dare I add, *eager* to be scammed."

"It's just possible that you're wrong about her, Jen."

She gave a dark laugh. "You know, Tori Spelling could be telling the truth when she says she got cast in *90210* without anyone knowing she's Aaron's daughter. But I doubt it."

Dawson lined up the shot and gave Jen the nod. She called action. Courtney broke into over-the-top, patently fake, hysterical sobbing.

"Cut!" Dawson called. He hurried over to Courtney.

"That wasn't what you wanted?" she asked.

"Try keeping it more internal," Dawson suggested. "Don't force things you don't feel. The camera can tell."

"Right. I understand totally," Courtney agreed.

The scene ran only eighty seconds, but Courtney was so awful that they did take after take after take. Drake was clearly getting exasperated. And Courtney's acting was, if anything, getting worse.

"Maybe we need to give this one a rest and come back to it," Dawson finally told Jen.

"That's not the problem, Dawson, and you know it," Jen said. "The problem is that Courtney deeply sucks."

"I think it's my fault, really," Dawson said. "I shouldn't have started with such an emotional scene."

"You shouldn't have cast such a crappy actress."

"Courtney will surprise you, Jen. Give her a chance."

"You are unbelievably gullible, Dawson." She sighed. "Okay. What scene do you think would make Sarah Bernhardt over there more comfortable?"

"The picnic," Dawson decided.

"Your wish is my command. Take twenty, everyone!" Jen yelled. "We're setting up for scene 15-C, the picnic!"

Dawson put his hand on her arm. "Thanks, Jen," he said. "I mean it."

"I mean it, too, Dawson. Courtney is an incendiary chick. And you're the one who's gonna get burned."

"Hi, mind if I join you?" Courtney settled down next to Pacey under the tree. She'd changed into the bathing suit she'd be wearing in the picnic scene, and her low-cut bikini top was clearly visible under her gauzy shirt—which was clearly the whole point.

"Not at all," Pacey said, careful to look everywhere except at what was on display. Andie was helping to set up the picnic props. If she saw him ogling Courtney's impressive cleavage, Andie would not be a happy camper.

There was a large cooler of lemonade next to him, compliments of Grams. "Care for some lemonade?" he asked.

"No, thanks. If I drink too much, I might have to run to the bathroom in the middle and keep everyone waiting."

"Very considerate," Pacey said, nodding.

"I try." She looked down at her chest. "You don't think this suit is too revealing for Dulcie, do you?"

"Fashion isn't exactly my strong suit," Pacey replied, though it was now even more difficult to keep his eyes off her chest.

"Well, Dawson said I should wear whatever bathing suit I felt comfortable in. And all my other bikini tops are much skimpier than this one. What could I do?"

The visual possibilities of that were almost too much for Pacey to contemplate.

Courtney leaned back on the palms of her hands.

"So, Pacey. What's this I hear about your grand passion to win the marathon kissing contest at the Romance Festival?"

"Who told you about that?"

Courtney laughed. "Maybe I'm psychic. You desperately want to win the Viper-for-a-week, true?"

"Is it true that I want to win? Yes. Is it true that I'm going to win? No."

"No?" She gave him an impish grin. "You look like a man whose lips would know how to participate."

"Thanks—I think. The problem is that my girlfriend's lips don't want to participate with me."

"Andie, you mean?" Courtney cast a quick look at Andie, who was scattering rose petals over the picnic blanket for the upcoming scene.

"Andie, I mean," Pacey agreed. "How did you know?"

"Pacey, Capeside is a pretty small place," Courtney said, laughing. "It's easy to find out everything about everyone in about twenty-four hours. So, are you madly in love with her?"

Pacey folded his arms and cocked his head at her. "Why do I feel like I'm being interviewed for a tell-all article for a trashy tabloid that doesn't realize it should have zero interest in my decidedly untrashy love life?"

"You know how those papers are," Courtney said. "They like to print titillating stuff that gets people excited." She leaned toward him. "Is your love life exciting, Pacey?"

"Is yours?" he countered.

She smiled. "I asked first."

"And the appropriate, mature answer would be, 'My love life is private.' "

"Good answer." Courtney drew her knees up to her chest, which did things to her bathing suit top that caused a serious lump in his throat and some other body parts.

"But you know what I don't get, Pacey?" Courtney went on. "If you and Andie are so hot together and so much in love, and she knows how much it means to you, why won't she enter the kissing contest with you?"

"Alas, even the perfect devotion of Andie McPhee has its limits." He put his hands behind his head. "What can you do?"

Courtney shrugged. "How about a different partner?"

Pacey laughed. "Right. That's a good one."

"I'm serious," Courtney insisted. "Why should you be deprived of winning just because she doesn't want to enter?"

"Why is because if my lips were glued to lips other than Andie's for the requisite twenty-nine hours and seven minutes it would take to win, she would rip my lips off my face immediately thereafter."

"But it's not real kissing," Courtney exclaimed. "It's a game. A contest! She can't possibly be that jealous and insecure, can she?"

"That strikes me as a very loaded question."

"Well, I think you're underestimating your girlfriend," Courtney said. "She loves you. So she'd want you to win that Viper, if that's what would make you happy."

"Possibly," Pacey allowed. "But the point is moot,

as they say on Court TV. I lack an alternative partner."

"How about me?" Courtney asked. "I know how to kiss."

"Good one," Pacey guffawed.

"I'm serious. I'd do it just to help you out," Courtney said.

"The question 'Why?' springs to mind," Pacey said.

Courtney thought for a moment. "Because I want to make up for how I treated you in New York." She playfully nudged her shoulder into his. "And because you're a nice guy, Pacey. You deserve to drive that Viper for a week."

"I agree. And thanks for the dream offer. If I thought for even a moment that you were serious, I might entertain the notion."

"I *am* serious."

Her blue eyes held his with a look so hot that Pacey was afraid smoke might start to pour from his ears. If he sat next to her for one more moment, someone was going to have to hose him down.

He jumped to his feet. "Hey, it was jive kidding around with you, really, but I gotta go." He shoved his hands deep into his pockets and began to back away from her.

"Think about what I said," Courtney called.

"Right. I'll do that." He gave her a mock salute, turned, and took off. Not that he had anywhere to go. But at the moment, being anywhere near Jen's cousin felt like a really dangerous place to be.

Chapter 7

Dawson lay on his bed, staring up at the ceiling. Streaks of light from the bright full moon shone on his troubled face. Make that deeply troubled. Because he had a major-league, deeply troubling problem.

Which was this: as an actress, Courtney sucked.

He had just reviewed everything he'd shot that day, and she had sucked in every single frame of it. Even when she managed to keep her mouth closed, her movements were reminiscent of some not very talented silent-film star telegraphing her emotions to the camera.

And he had no idea what to do about it. He'd tried everything, but no matter what approach he took, she didn't respond to his direction.

Maybe Jen was right, and he had made a mistake by casting her. Drake certainly thought so. When they'd wrapped for the day, he had taken Dawson aside and told him that basically Courtney was ruining the film, and if Dawson had a brain he'd fire her and hire Joey. Jen just happened to amble over to offer her unvarnished agreement.

Dawson hadn't reacted well to it. Okay, so maybe he had gotten a little defensive, with both of them laying into him like that, so sure that he was wrong about the casting of *his* film. He'd insisted to them that Courtney was his vision of Dulcie, and if it wasn't working it was his fault, because he hadn't yet found the right way to direct her.

Dawson only hoped his rationalization hid some actual truth.

As he lay there, Joey popped into his mind, which wasn't unusual. But now he saw Joey as Dulcie. Kissing Drake/Don. Over and over and over. Dawson shuddered at the thought.

Joey hadn't been upset when she wasn't cast—it wasn't as though she had any confidence in herself as an actress. She did, however, think Dawson had lost whatever small amount of sanity he'd ever possessed by casting "that psycho rich-witch, Courtney," as she had so undiplomatically put it.

He had to prove her—all of them—wrong. And he had to save his film.

Desperation spurred him to action. He got off his bed, pulled on a sweatshirt, and headed next door. He had to talk to Courtney, find a way to get her to relax, to trust him and herself, to—

"Dawson, hi!" Courtney said from the other side of the screen door of Grams' house, just as Dawson had been about to ring the doorbell.

"I know it's late to be stopping over," he said. "I was hoping we could talk."

She laughed. "It's not ten o'clock yet, Dawson. In New York, you don't dare show your face at a club before eleven."

She came outside and joined him on the doorstep. "I'm really glad you're here. Actually, I was thinking about coming over to your house, because I wanted to talk to you, too. But I didn't know what time your folks go to sleep. And I didn't want to climb in your window. In case you weren't alone."

"I seem to be quite alone these days," Dawson admitted.

Her eyebrows rose in surprise. "That's hard to believe. I thought you and Joey—?"

"We were," Dawson said. "And we might be again. But for now we're . . . not."

She touched his arm lightly, her eyes filled with compassion. "I'm sorry. I mean, from what I heard, you really do love Joey. And I know Jen kind of complicated that for you."

"I didn't come to talk about Joey, Courtney. Or Jen, for that matter. Could we—?" He motioned to the dock down at the creek.

"Sure."

They walked together to the dock and sat on the edge of it, their knees almost touching. The gentle sounds of katydids and crickets filled the night air. Out in the channel, a big striped bass chasing some mullet exploded from the water, its black and white markings gleaming in the moonlight.

Courtney inhaled deeply. "I love the way the air smells here. So fresh. And that full moon. You never even notice a full moon in New York. Too many bright lights twenty-four/seven."

Dawson nodded. Now that he was with her, he had no idea how to begin. "So . . . why were you going to come see me?" he finally asked.

"Probably the same reason you came over here. I want to be honest with you, Dawson." She turned to him. "I don't think I was very good today."

"You don't?"

"No. And you don't think I was very good, either," Courtney said. "I know I can do better! It's just that . . ."

"What? I'll help you any way that I can, Courtney."

She nibbled on her lower lip. "Are you sure I can confide in you?"

"Of course, I'm the director. It's my job to bring out the best performance in the actors."

She nodded solemnly. "Well, for one thing, I know Jen doesn't think you should have cast me. You know how straightforward she is—she came right out and told me."

"She shouldn't have done that."

"No, it's okay," Courtney insisted, lightly resting her left hand on his right one. "I respect her for it. I mean, she's always been so sure of herself, so confident. Today, every time she called 'stand by,' I felt like she was just waiting for me to mess up." She hung her head, her hair a blond veil over her eyes. "The truth is, she's always kind of intimidated me, Dawson. And I suppose in the past I've compensated for that by not being as nice to her as I should be. It's not something I'm proud of."

"Maybe you should tell her that sometime," Dawson suggested.

"I know, I should, but . . . it's hard."

"Jen is—" Dawson stopped, searching for the right words. "I care about her a lot. She's much more vulnerable than you realize. And smart and talented. And she's completely committed to the success of the film."

"Committed to the film's success, yes," Courtney said softly. She raised her head, her hair fell away from her face, and Dawson saw tears in her luminous eyes. "But not committed to my success."

"It's possible that her animosity toward you is somewhat coloring her attitude toward your work," Dawson allowed. "I could talk to her."

"Would you? That would be wonderful. And there's one other thing." Courtney hesitated, exhaled audibly. "Wow, this one is really hard to say."

Dawson waited.

"The thing is, I know that *Don and Dulcie* came from your heart, Dawson. It's . . . well, it's brilliant. When I auditioned with you in your bedroom, and you were Don, I really *felt* Dulcie. But Drake just doesn't have your heart, or your soul. I just don't feel it with him."

Her eyes shone at him in the moonlight. She looked lovely, and very vulnerable.

"I appreciate your honesty, Courtney. And . . . well, frankly, I'm flattered. I should point out that you don't really know me. In fact it's likely that you've assigned certain positive qualities to me because of the nature of the script—qualities that I might or might not even possess."

"You see, that is so you, Dawson. You don't even want to take credit for how wonderful you are."

"I . . . I'm a little uncomfortable with this, actually," he admitted. "That is, I—"

She put her hand on his arm. "It's okay. I understand. But as my director, let me ask you. Do you think it would be terrible if I pretend that Drake is you?"

Dawson felt the color rising to his cheeks. "Terrible? No, not terrible. Not at all terrible. Not if you find it helpful, that is." He knew he was stammering like an idiot, but he couldn't seem to help himself.

"Good." She beamed at him. "Wow, I feel so much better! Oh, I have a great idea!"

"What's that?"

"If I'm having trouble with a certain scene, maybe we could work on it privately. You know, you could play Don again. That would help me so much."

"If you think—"

"I do." She threw her arms around his neck and hugged him. "Thank you, Dawson. For being so supportive."

Slowly, she pulled away. But not very far away. She stared up at him, her lips slightly parted, as if she wanted him to kiss her.

Well, why not? He was a free agent these days. Supposedly.

And it certainly wouldn't be the first time that a director and his leading lady had begun a romance.

"Dawson," she whispered huskily. Her lips were almost on his.

Some impulse made him pull away. He stood up.

"Well, I'm glad we talked, Courtney. I feel much better about everything."

She stood up, too. "Me, too." A lazy half grin curved her lips. "I don't know if I'm going to sleep very well, though. I have a feeling you're going to be in my dreams. And you won't be acting."

". . . And talking with Dawson really helped me, Jen," Courtney was saying as they walked into the Baskin-Robbins near the beach a half hour later. "I just know I'm going to really be able to get into my character tomorrow."

"Good," Jen replied. "I hope you're right." It was all she could do to refrain from telling Courtney that she could do Dawson and the entire town of Capeside a favor by dropping out of the film, and then dropping out of Capeside.

Right after Dawson had left, Jen had wandered downstairs to find Courtney coming back to the house from her talk with Dawson. Both girls were still wound up from working on the movie all day, so they decided to go for a drive to get ice cream. The Baskin-Robbins was one of the few places in Capeside that was open past ten.

"One double-dip cone with chocolate chip ice cream, please," Jen ordered from the woman behind the counter, who wore a huge button that read "Capeside *Is* Romance," with the dates of the Capeside Romance Festival underneath.

"I'll have a sugar-free, fat-free vanilla cup, please. Small. With a small spoon, please," Courtney ordered.

"Figures," Jen mumbled under her breath.

"I heard that, Jen," Courtney said sweetly, as the woman behind the counter filled their orders. "Small spoons fool your stomach into thinking you're eating more. You wouldn't want a fat Dulcie, would you?"

"Actually, I think the whole point of the film is that to Don, Dulcie is beautiful, no matter what."

"Which is a beautiful sentiment, really," Courtney said. "Not that anyone actually believes it, of course."

"Dawson does," Jen said. "Well, at least he *thinks* he does."

They paid for their ice cream and went to sit at one of the small tables outside.

"This is so great." Courtney spooned some ice cream into her mouth. "It's so peaceful here. No smog, no crime. On top of that, Drake Keller, all to myself."

Jen shot her a sharp look. "What is that supposed to mean? You only went out with the guy once."

"Surely you haven't been away from the big city for so long that you've forgotten all the rules of the game, Jen," Courtney said. "I'm playing hard to get."

"Right," Jen snorted. "Only he isn't playing with you." Jen liked Drake, and frankly, it irked her to think that he might actually be into Courtney. As far as *Don and Dulcie* went, so far he'd been totally attitude-free. You'd never know that he was a professional actor who lived in Los Angeles. He had gone out of his way to make everyone feel comfortable. On top of that, he really was talented. Not to mention gorgeous.

"Oh, Jen, come on," Courtney chided, "you know me. I can get any guy I want."

"This may be a difficult concept for you to grasp, Courtney," Jen began, "but guys are people. They aren't possessions, and you don't *get* them like you *get* whatever you want by pulling out your credit card at Bloomingdale's."

Courtney licked some ice cream off her tiny spoon. "You're right," she agreed. "With guys, it's free. Besides, what happened to the Jen who used to collect guys like some girls collect MAC lip liners?"

"I left her in New York," Jen said.

Courtney nodded. "I understand. You came here to reinvent yourself. It's admirable, really. I can see how hard you're trying to fit in here."

"I *do* fit in here."

"And you've made some really great friends here, I know. They care about you a lot." Courtney rewound her hair into a messy bun. "And I know it hurts them as much as it hurts me to hear people in Capeside talking about you like you're some slut." She pitched the last half of her ice cream into the nearby trash barrel.

Jen's jaw set. "What are you talking about?"

"Forget it," Courtney said quickly. "I shouldn't have said anything."

"You're right, you shouldn't have. Now tell me what you're talking about."

Courtney got up. "Forget it, Jen, really. Let's go—"

Jen grabbed her cousin's arm hard. "No, let's not forget it. God, you're so transparent. You throw a punch, aim at my gut, make sure you score, then

84

pretend you never meant to hit me. Now, you *will* tell me what you meant."

Courtney sighed. "Okay, but you're forcing this, not me. Drake told me he heard you'd had sex with everything in Capeside that zips at the crotch."

Jen felt like she couldn't breathe. "Congratulations, Courtney," she managed. "First you got me on the ropes, then you knocked me out in the first round."

"I didn't want to tell you, Jen—"

"Of course you didn't *want* to tell me. You were *dying* to tell me. And you know what makes you so amazing, Courtney? Even though I can tell myself that you probably made the whole thing up just to make me feel exactly like I'm feeling right now, I can't be sure. And you know it."

Courtney's eyes filled with tears. "Jen, I'm so sorry. Really. Sometimes I just have the biggest mouth."

"Hey, ladies, out savoring that hot Capeside night life?" Pacey called, as he rode by on his bike.

He circled back over to them, and Jen took the opportunity to calm herself down. After all, the worse she felt, the more she was letting Courtney win.

"Hi, Pacey," Courtney said. "Nice bike."

"Yeah, well, my Viper is in the shop." He stopped, straddling his bike. "Andie and I were out cruising, but she decided to pack it in after I whined for about an hour about her not entering the kissing contest with me."

"Andie won't budge on it, huh?" Jen asked sympathetically.

"Not a millimeter," Pacey said. "Not even my manly recitation of a love poem—which, by the way, I committed to memory on her behalf—coerced her to change her mind."

"But that's so sweet!" Courtney cried. "If the guy I loved ever memorized a love poem for me, I'd be putty in his hands."

"Interesting image," Pacey mused. "Anyway, Andie is not the moldable type."

"And more power to her, I say," Jen said. She looked at her watch. "I'm heading back, Courtney. You've got a seven o'clock call, and I have to meet Dawson at six-thirty."

"Oh, you go ahead," Courtney said. "You know I don't need much sleep." She turned to Pacey. "I used to party at the clubs until three-thirty, then get up at six for school."

"*Used* to?" Jen commented nastily.

"And just out of curiosity, how did you get in the clubs, anyway?" Pacey asked. "Don't you have to be twenty-one or something?"

Courtney laughed. "You're kidding, right?"

"Wrong."

"Come on, tell me you don't have fake ID, Pacey," Courtney said.

"Okay. I don't have fake ID."

She kissed his cheek. "That is so sweet. I'll get you some. My treat."

Jen rolled her eyes. "I'm gone," she told them, walking away. Then she called over her shoulder, "Don't worry about walking home by yourself, Courtney. The most dangerous person in Capeside is probably you."

"Ouch." Pacey gave Courtney a quizzical look.

"Oh, she's mad about something I told her," Courtney explained. Her face lit up suddenly. "Hey, know what I'd love to do? Take a walk on the beach."

"Yeah? Cool, have fun," Pacey said.

"I meant with you, silly," Courtney laughed.

"With me." Pacey just stood there, straddling his bike. "Uh . . . I don't know if that's such a good idea."

Courtney stuck out her lower lip in a babyish pout. "But it's no fun to do it by myself. Please?"

"I don't know . . ." Pacey wavered.

"Don't worry, Pacey," Courtney said. "As cute as you are, I know you're in love with Andie. I would never poach on another girl's guy."

"Good." Pacey got off his bike and rolled it over to a tree. "Not that I'm poachable, by the by. Although I should mention that all efforts in that direction will be treated as a boon to my pathetically frail ego."

"You are so funny," she said as she grabbed his arm when they reached the ocean. Courtney splashed into the shallow water, whooping at the top of her lungs. "This is so great! I love it here."

From the beach, Pacey called back to her. "Trust me, as a permanent residence the luster wears thin."

She splashed around some more, then joined him on the beach. They walked along the water line slowly, in companionable silence.

Courtney glanced at him. "Andie is a lucky girl."

"Actually, she's gone through a lot of rough stuff

with her family that no one could possibly construe as lucky."

She playfully bumped her shoulder into his as they walked along. "I meant that she's lucky to have you, silly boy."

Pacey let that one sink in for a moment. "Right. I knew that."

"You *should* know it, but I don't think you really do," Courtney said. "I just have this feeling that you're one of those guys who is so fantastic—smart, funny, sexy—and you're blind to it."

"Funny how every woman in Capeside shares that particular lack of vision. Except Andie, that is."

"That is so not true," Courtney insisted. She stopped and bent down to pick up a scallop shell. "I happen to know lots of girls in Capeside who think you're hot."

Pacey folded his arms. "Just out of curiosity, who?"

She stood up, brushing sand off her shell. "Me."

Pacey ran his hand through his hair. "Yeah?"

"I wouldn't say it if it wasn't true." She looked him in the eye. "I meant what I told you this afternoon, you know. If Andie really loves you, I don't understand why she won't be in the kissing contest with you."

"I don't understand, either, actually," Pacey admitted.

"Well," Courtney said with a shrug, "don't be too hard on her. I really like Andie. And maybe it has something to do with her emotional problems."

"How do you know about that?" Pacey asked sharply.

Courtney shook her head sadly. "It's really terrible how people spread rumors in a small town. And anyway, Pacey, it's no big thing. All my friends are on Prozac. In New York, if you're not crazy and in therapy, everyone *really* thinks you're crazy."

"Charming. Well, maybe we ought to be going—"

"Wait." She put her hand on his arm. "I just wanted to tell you one last thing. I meant something else I told you this afternoon. I really will be in the kissing contest with you."

Pacey mimed shifting gears. "I can almost feel that Viper power in my hands."

Courtney smiled. "We'd win, you know. Believe me."

"Somehow, I do. However, I have a feeling it was just not meant to be."

"Well, maybe you need something to change that feeling. You know what they say, feeling is believing."

Before Pacey knew what was happening, she was in his arms, kissing him passionately.

Chapter 8

"**O**kay, that's a wrap for today," Jen told the weary-looking group of actors and techies who were assembled on the creek bank. "Tomorrow's call is for eight o'clock, just outside the Ice House. Thanks, everybody."

Jen rubbed between her eyes. They had just finished the second day of shooting *Don and Dulcie*, and she had a vicious headache. For one thing, she couldn't seem to let go of what Courtney had told her the night before. All her conversations with Drake were terse, bordering on rude.

Logically, she knew Courtney's story—that Drake said he'd heard Jen was the slut of Capeside—was probably invented by Courtney to make Jen feel like crap. But the fact was, there was enough doubt in Jen's mind to think it could possibly be true. And Courtney had succeeded in making her feel likc crap.

Both these facts only made her feel crappier.

And if that wasn't bad enough, Courtney's acting had, if possible, deteriorated overnight. She was flat-out hopeless. Even the extras and the crew were whispering about it. Only Dawson had seemed not to have noticed.

Everyone was exhausted and irritable from doing take after take that never got any better. Yes, they all liked Courtney. She was unfailingly nice to everyone. But as an actress, hey, the girl bit the big one.

Jen peered through the crowd of volunteers tearing down the day's set, looking for Dawson. He was at the props table, deep in conversation with Courtney. And he kept nodding at whatever it was she was saying.

"Where do you want the props for tomorrow stored?" Andie called to Jen.

"Put them in the back of Chris' truck, thanks," Jen told her. "Be sure to check them off the master list, Andie."

"Got it," Andie assured her.

Someone tapped her on the shoulder. Jen turned around.

It was Drake.

"Can I speak with you a minute?" he asked her.

"Sure," she said briskly, her guard going up immediately. "What's up?"

He regarded her thoughtfully for a moment. "Listen, did I do something to piss you off?"

"No, why?"

"Maybe it's just me, then."

"Maybe," she agreed, trying to bluster her way through the conversation. "So, is that all?"

He hesitated. "I guess I just thought we had the beginnings of . . . I don't know. Something."

That hit Jen like yet another fist in her stomach. He had heard she put out, and he wanted some action, too. No, that was way too paranoid.

But what if it was true?

"I'm just a little preoccupied right now," she said. "Don't take it personally."

He gave her a wry look. "Well, see, the thing is, I *want* to take it personally. I thought maybe you did, too."

"It's like this," Jen began. "I feel a lot of pressure to do a great job producing this film. So I'm not really thinking about anything else right now. Or any*one* else."

"Okay," Drake said reluctantly. "I can deal. We'll keep it business, if that's the way you want it."

"That's the way it is. Besides, I thought you were going out with Courtney," Jen couldn't help adding.

"Oh, so that's what this is about!" He smacked himself in the forehead with the palm of his hand. "You think I'm dating your cousin and hitting on you at the same time. No wonder you—"

"Look, I don't think anything, okay? I just—"

"Jen, I'm not dating Courtney. It's true she called me one night and asked me to hang out with her, and I did. But that's it. Nothing happened. And frankly, I have zero interest in her." He shoved his hands into the pockets of his jeans.

The look on his face was so guileless that Jen almost believed him. Almost.

"Courtney doesn't seem to see it that way, apparently," she said, and began to gather up her notes, pens, and various clipboards.

Drake knelt down to help her. "I can't be responsible for what she sees or how she sees it. But if you think you're dissing your cousin by going out with me, you're not."

Their eyes met. "Who said anything about going out with you?" Jen asked.

He looked bewildered. "I thought that's what we were just talking about."

"You were asking me out?"

He laughed. "Don't people do that kind of thing in Capeside?"

"It's been known to happen." They both stood up.

"So, let me formally ask you out, then," Drake said through an ironic smile. "Jen, would you go out with me Saturday night?"

God, he was cute. And nice. Really, really nice. Maybe he had heard rumors about her, maybe he hadn't. But it wasn't like she couldn't handle herself around him, either way.

"Okay," she decided.

His face broke into a grin. "That's a yes?"

She laughed. "Yes, that's a yes."

"Great. I'll try to come up with something great to do. Unless you had something in mind?"

"Capside will be teeming with tourists for the festival. I've sort of ignored the schedule of events."

"I'll check it out, then. Just one other thing."

What? Bring birth control?

"What?" she asked warily.

"About Courtney," Drake said, folding his arms

and frowning. "Jen, she reeked worse today than she did yesterday. I know how cheesy it is for one actor to complain about another actor, but—"

"You're preaching to the choir, Drake," Jen interrupted. "It's Dawson we have to convince."

They both looked at Dawson, who was still deep in conversation with Courtney.

"How can the guy not know how bad she is?" Drake wondered, his eyes still on Courtney and Dawson. "Unless he's doing her."

Jen gave a sharp laugh. "Trust me. Dawson Leery is not having sex with my cousin. Dawson is not a guy who thinks with his crotch. He's more a heart man . . . an organ which my cousin does not possess."

Drake gave her an appraising look. "Oh, so that's her deal."

"Think Jennifer Jason Leigh in *Single White Female* and you pretty much have the gist." She glanced at Dawson again. Courtney had thrown her arms around his neck. She kissed him softly on the cheek and then waved good-bye, walking over to Chris Wolfe's little sister Dina, of all people.

She turned to Drake. "Let's go talk to Dawson."

"Yeah?"

"Come on," Jen said.

Dawson saw them coming. He put his palms up to him. "I know what the two of you are about to say. I know Courtney's work today was not exactly excellent, but—"

"Dawson, getting up in the morning to go to high school is 'not exactly excellent,' " Jen said. "Court-ney's work today was more, say, on the level of abysmal. Horrendous. Excruciating. Appalling. Shall I go on?"

"Please, don't hold back just because I cast her and I believe in her," Dawson said sarcastically.

"Maybe you're too close to it or something," Drake suggested. "Her work today didn't get better. It got worse."

"I'm aware of that," Dawson said stiffly.

"What I don't understand—and pardon me if I'm overstepping my bounds as an actor, here," Drake added, "but what I don't understand is why you don't fire Courtney and hire that girl Joey instead. She was really good."

"No offense, Drake, but you *are* kind of overstepping your bounds, here," Dawson said.

Jen shook her head. "What is up with you, Dawson? How can you be so willing to screw up your own film? You want Courtney's work to be preserved for the next millennium? It doesn't make any sense. Are you that threatened by the idea of Joey and Drake—"

"It's not about that," Dawson said. The tension in his voice was palpable.

"So what *is* it about, then?" Jen demanded.

Dawson waited a beat, a muscle working in his jaw. "All right, I'll tell you, Jen. Since you clearly want this movie to succeed, you should know what's getting in Courtney's way. She feels that you're not being supportive of her work."

"*What?*" Jen exploded.

"Look, I know this is awkward," Dawson said. "But we're all on the same side here. And if your personal animosity toward her is making her feel tense in front of the camera, then that's something we have to deal with."

Jen was incredulous. "She actually sold you on that pile of puke, Dawson? And you *believed* her?"

"The point isn't whether I believe her or not," Dawson doggedly insisted. "If it's what she believes, even if the truth is of an utterly different nature, then it's essential that we deal with it for the good of the project."

"Let's all break into a chorus of 'Isn't It Ironic?' shall we?" Jen sneered. "Courtney is playing you big time, Dawson. And you don't see it because it happens to play right into your own needs and insecurities."

"Listen, man, for the good of your film—" Drake began.

Dawson turned on him. "While I appreciate that you care about the good of my film, Drake, this really doesn't concern you."

"Yeah, it does," Drake said. "I'm sorry, but I can't afford to have some piece of crap floating around out there with me in it. You never know who could end up seeing it, and that's not a risk I'm willing to take."

Dawson gave him a level gaze. "Which means?"

"Which means I agreed to be in your film because I think your script is really good," Drake said. "I thought it would be a fun thing to do while I'm in Capeside. But Courtney's acting is so rank that she's wrecking the art *and* the fun. So although I am not usually an ultimatum kind of guy, if you don't replace her with Joey, I'm gone."

With a final look to Jen that seemed to express his regret, he took off.

"Unbelievable," Dawson seethed. "And he calls himself a professional! He made a commitment, and he knows we have two days of film in the can, but, hey, too bad; if I don't get my own way, I drop out?"

"Come on, Dawson," Jen chided. "You know none of the scenes with Courtney are usable. Drake's right."

"Fine," Dawson said gruffly.

She knew that underneath Dawson's anger, he felt incredibly hurt. And she couldn't help it, it hurt her to hurt him, even though she knew she was right. She reached for his hand. "Dawson—"

He pulled away. "I really need you to leave me alone right now, Jen."

"All right," Jen said. "I'll be home, if you want to talk, okay?"

He didn't answer.

An hour later, Jen was ringing Joey's doorbell. No answer. Between two strips of badly peeling paint on the door, she noticed a small sign: "Bell Broken, Knock Loud."

She banged her fist on the door and waited. When she'd stopped at the Ice House, Bessie had told her she thought Joey was home working on an art project. Jen had thought about calling first, then decided to just show up.

Some things were better done face to face.

When no one came to the door, Jen kicked the base of the door, making as much noise as possible.

She'd rowed all the way across the creek—it was worth one last shot.

"Jeez, don't break the door down!" Joey yelled from inside the house. A few moments later, she opened the door, peering at Jen with surprise. "Let me guess," she said. "Your grandmother finally won you over, and you've come by to save my soul."

"That would be rather ironic, don't you think?"

"Yes, actually I do," Joey admitted.

"Can I come in?"

Wordlessly, Joey ushered Jen inside and into the small, shabby living room. Alexander's baby toys were scattered everywhere. There was a slice of burnt toast on the scarred coffee table, and another on the carpet underneath it. A baby bottle of orange juice had leaked on the couch cushions.

"I haven't had time to play Merry Maid yet today," Joey said defensively. She began to straighten things up. "I've been trying to finish this project for my art class, and—"

"You don't owe me any explanations," Jen said.

"You're right, I don't." Joey looked at her arms, full of dirty dishes and baby toys. She dropped the toys into Alexander's playpen and took the dishes into the kitchen.

When she came back, Jen was sitting on the couch. "So, to what do I owe this unannounced, unplanned-for visit?"

"Dawson needs you," Jen said bluntly.

"Excuse me?"

"It's like this. As a human being, my cousin Courtney ranks somewhere below the sixth rung of Hell. And as an actress, she ranks even lower than that."

Joey sat down on the couch. "What does that have to do with me?"

"You gave, by far, the best audition for Dulcie. Everyone knows it, including me, including Drake."

"And *ex*cluding Dawson," Joey said. "He cast Courtney. It's his movie. End of story."

"Dawson is currently in his stubborn-pigheaded-egocentric-I-can't-admit-I-made-a-mistake mode," Jen explained. "But underneath that, he knows you're the best actress for Dulcie, too."

Joey thought a minute. "If that's so—which I highly doubt—then he'll have to tell me so himself."

"But you see, that's just the point, Joey," Jen said. "He can't bring himself to do it, even though he knows it's what he should do."

Joey shrugged. "You're his producer, not me. Deal with it."

"I *am* dealing with it," Jen explained in exasperation. "That's why I'm here." She sighed and raked a hand through her hair. "This is how it is, Joey. Dawson likes me. Maybe he even likes me a lot. And he probably lusts after me a lot."

Joey folded her arms. "Your point?"

"My point is that I'm acutely aware of the fact that he's not in love with me. Because he's still in love with someone else, and we both know it, even if that someone else is not his at the moment. Sometimes I think it's precisely *because* that someone else isn't his at the moment."

"What does this have to do with—"

"His film," Jen put in. "It's just this. The idea of watching you do love scenes with Drake is so painful to him that he's willing to let Courtney ruin his film rather than fire her and hire you. He won't admit that, of course—not even to himself. But if Dawson doesn't replace Courtney with you, Drake is walking. And then Dawson can kiss his film good-bye."

Joey twisted the tie of her drawstring pants between her fingers. "So wonderful Jen comes to the rescue, is that it? You're saving Dawson from himself?"

"I'm trying to save his movie," Jen said. "I thought that might interest you. But evidently I thought wrong." She got up and headed for the door.

"Wait," Joey called. "I . . . God, why is it that you bring out the very worst in me?"

"Write to 'Hey, Cherie!' at the newspaper and ask her, not me," Jen said sarcastically.

"Okay, I deserve that," Joey allowed. "Did I really give a good audition? I'm just . . . it's not like I was any good in Dawson's earlier movies."

"What possible reason could I have to lie to you about it?" Jen asked.

"To get back at your witchy cousin?" Joey suggested.

"Granted, that concept does give me a certain satisfaction," Jen admitted. "But I'd never try to replace her unless she was really wrecking the film, and I think, deep down, you know that. Besides, it's not exactly in my best interests to ask you to be Dawson's leading lady."

"Point taken. So, what is it that you want me to do?"

"You know the scene by the creek, where Don

sees Dulcie for the first time? I want you and Drake to do that scene tonight. For Dawson. If Dawson buys into it, he saves his movie. If he doesn't . . . well, then he doesn't."

Joey looked down at one of her sandals and scuffed it into the worn carpet. "True confession time, Jen: right now, you are a better friend to Dawson than I am."

She looked up, and their eyes locked.

"I know," Jen said.

Chapter 9

Dawson checked his viewfinder again, then turned to talk to Courtney.

"Right before the kiss, Courtney, I think Drake needs more of a yearning quality. We have to be able to feel it even when he isn't speaking."

"Got it." Courtney dutifully wrote Dawson's instructions in her notebook. "I'll make sure Drake gets the note."

He smiled at her.

Dawson simply could not believe how nice she had been about getting the ax. The night before, as he was once again wearing out his bedroom carpet trying to figure out how to save his movie, Jen had called. She said it was crucial that he meet her down by the creek at ten, but refused to say why.

He went. Only, when he got there, it wasn't just Jen waiting for him. There was Drake, too.

And Joey.

"Don't worry, Dawson," Joey had said, clearly covering her own discomfort. "This is not a *Bob and Carol and Ted and Alice* moment."

Ha. Trust Joey to go for a classic movie title about two couples who swap partners. How not amusing.

Jen had quickly explained that she'd asked Drake and Joey to do the creek scene for him in the real environment. All she was asking was that Dawson watch with an open mind. Then he could make his own decision.

Ambushed. But Dawson had dutifully watched the scene.

It was amazing.

Drake and Joey *were* Don and Dulcie. The scene came to life and sizzled with all the heat he'd envisioned, even in the harsh makeshift lighting Jen had set up. The scene gave him that same rush he'd gotten when he'd stayed up all night writing the screenplay in the first place: the rush of an artistic high of monumental proportions.

No way could he turn away from that. Not even if it meant admitting he was wrong. Not even if it meant firing Courtney.

Not even if it meant having to watch Joey sizzle with Drake.

Oh, God.

But Dawson was resolved to do what he had to do. So he'd asked Courtney to go for a walk with him. It wasn't Courtney's fault, he'd explained. It was entirely his fault, for lacking the ability to tap into the talent he knew was inside of her.

So he had to replace her.

He'd been prepared for fireworks. Or waterworks. Or both. But instead, she had apologized to him, saying that it wasn't his fault at all, but hers. Because she had been unable to create her character knowing that Jen was judging her every move. That had just felt too vulnerable, and she was so sorry she had let Dawson down.

And *then* she had volunteered to be his assistant, because she really felt she had so much to learn from him.

What an amazing girl.

It was now late afternoon, and all day Courtney had been right there to help him and Jen in every way. As for Joey, she was doing an awesome job in the role of Dulcie. From an artistic point of view, Dawson was flying. But every time he watched some passionate or tender moment between Drake and Joey, it caused him acute physical pain.

Courtney was right there to tend his wounds.

"Anything else?" Courtney asked now, her pen poised.

"Just that I want to tell you again how much help you've been to me today, and how amazing your attitude is," Dawson said. "I know you said you wanted to learn from me, but actually I think I could learn a lot from you. About the proportionality of ego in art, for example."

"Here, Courtney," little Dina said, handing a bottle of juice to the older girl. "And I got a straw. I know you like straws."

"You are the greatest," Courtney told her.

"Tell *him* that," Dina said, cocking her chin at Dawson.

"Remember our deal, Dina?" Dawson said. "You can help on the film if you forgo the endless insinuations that there is something personal going on between me and you."

She blinked at him coolly. "You know you want me."

Dawson made a noise of frustration as Courtney laughed and gave Dina a hug. "You're too cute, Dina. Trust me, he will want you one day. Now, can you do me the biggest favor and make sure Drake and Joey get some cold lemonade from that thermos on the food table?"

"Consider it done," Dina said with dignity, and took off for the refreshment table.

"Yo," Jen called as she strode over to them. "Ready to capture this for posterity? We're losing the light."

"Ready," Dawson said. He glanced at Joey, who was mumbling her lines to herself while Andie brushed powder on her face.

"Okay, places for scene 27, please, the final kiss at the creek!" Jen called.

Joey hurried over to the spot by the creek where Drake/Don would discover her.

Dawson nodded at Jen.

"And . . . action!" he called.

Joey/Dulcie began to skim one stone after another across the water. She had a faraway look in her eyes. Dawson's camera followed one stone as it skipped five times across the water, then came in for a close-up of Joey. The pain on her face was palpable. Her eyes filled with the tears that she would not allow to fall. She knew Don wasn't going to show up, that he had used her just like every other guy. How had she allowed herself to be so vulnerable? She, who had hardened her heart to—

She heard something behind her. Startled, she turned. Don came to her, and she slowly lifted her face up, just as Dawson directed. They stared into each other's eyes.

"Don't you know that you can't tilt at windmills?" Joey/Dulcie asked him. "Fairy tales don't come true. There are no happily-ever-afters."

His answer was to take her into his arms and kiss her with a tender passion that told her she was wrong.

"Cut!" Dawson called.

It took a moment for Joey and Drake to break apart. They both looked a little dazed. The crew broke into spontaneous applause and appreciative whistles.

"You can breathe now, Dawson," Jen said, gathering some more flat stones for Joey to toss so they could reshoot the scene from a different angle. "The lip lock is over."

Dawson busied himself with his camera.

"Jen doesn't understand how hard this is for you," Courtney murmured sympathetically near his right ear. "But I want you to know, Dawson. When I was in your arms, you made me feel exactly like Dulcie feels with Don."

Could that be true? Dawson didn't trust himself to speak. So he didn't.

Joey sat in the shade, sipping the lemonade Dina had brought her, while Andie redid her makeup.

"You know, you're really good at this," Andie said as she applied loose powder to Joey's face with a large brush.

"I think it's just some kind of weird aberration of the moment," Joey said, blowing some powder off her face. "Dawson practically had to force me and Pacey to be in his early cinematic efforts. To say I was pathetic would be kind. He even did a horror project; the scariest thing about that movie was my performance. "

"Well, maybe this role speaks to you," Andie said, handing Joey a mirror so she could check out her makeup. "You have to admit, Drake is to die for. I wouldn't mind playing his damsel in distress."

"It's acting, Andie," Joey insisted.

Andie gave her a jaded look. "Are you going to tell me that when Drake Keller takes you in his arms and kisses you, you feel absolutely nothing?"

"I wouldn't say I feel absolutely nothing," Joey admitted. "I might have some . . . purely biological reaction to his purely biological reaction."

"I knew it," Andie said.

"Andie, we have no interest in each other," Joey said. "He told me he asked Jen out and he really likes her, which is just fine by me." She peered at herself in the mirror. "Why do you have to wear so much makeup to make it look like you're not wearing any makeup?"

"I have no idea." Andie put the hand mirror away. "Listen, I'm completely aware that you and Drake are just playing a role. It's no different from *She's All That*. In the real world, the hottest, not to mention most sensitive guy in the entire school never does fall in love with Geek Girl. And Geek Girl never does just happen to have body-of-death hidden under her baggy clothes. And it's only in the movies that Hot Guy doesn't know or care about body-of-death but falls in love with Geek Girl's unblemished soul. Seriously delusional fantasy land, right? Right. But the whole point is to get carried away to fantasy land."

"Fantasy land of what?" Pacey asked, strolling over, two Cokes in hand. He gave one to Andie, who had gotten over being mad at him. Not that she'd changed her mind about the kissing contest. But at least they weren't at war over it anymore.

Andie took a sip of the Coke. "I was telling Joey that every time she and Drake kiss, I forget all over again that it isn't real. It's called suspension of disbelief."

"I suggest you not share that with Dawson," Pacey said. "It's one of those good-news-bad-news things. You know, good news that the scene is working. Bad news . . . well, the bad news is obvious."

"Jeez, I should make a recording," Joey said. "There's nothing going on between me and Drake."

"And yet there's a whole lot going on between Don and Dulcie," Pacey pointed out. "Let's just say Dawson's suffering a little suspension of disbelief in reverse."

"Dawson and I—" Joey began.

"—are not, at the present time, a dynamic duo in the romantic sense," Pacey recited. "Which I'm sure was a selfless act on your part to give the ever-precocious Dina a shot at the object of her affections."

Joey glanced over at Dawson, who was checking something on his camera as Courtney whispered in his ear. Courtney's hands had been all over Dawson all day long. And Dawson didn't exactly seem to be fighting it.

Drake walked over to join Joey. "Hey, I thought that last take went really well, didn't you?"

She shrugged. "You're the professional."

"You're doing a really great job. Jen thinks so, too—she just told me. Listen, just an observation, but you look like your shoulders are attached to your ears. May I?"

He lightly began to massage her shoulders, and Joey closed her eyes blissfully. "That feels really good. I didn't even realize I was so tense."

"That's where I hold all my tension, too," Drake said. "My fantasy is to have a masseuse on the set of any movie I'm lucky enough to get cast in. It really helps." He stopped massaging her, his hands resting lightly on her shoulders. "Better?"

"Much," she said, smiling at him. "Thanks."

Pacey looked at Dawson to see if he was taking in the massage parlor action, but Dawson was still talking with Courtney and wasn't even looking in their direction. Well, that was good. Because he knew Dawson was capable of construing an innocent shoulder rub right before his eyes as guilty foreplay.

Pacey watched Courtney write down something else Dawson told her. He had changed his opinion of her completely. She really was a great girl. Take what happened the other night, for example. After he'd gotten over the initial shock of having Courtney kissing him like that, he'd gently pulled away from her. Not that he wasn't flattered.

But his body was making dates that his mind did not intend to keep. Alas, Pacey Witter, former horned toad in training, was a one-woman man. And that woman's name was McPhee.

Courtney had said to him she'd only kissed him because, well, because she couldn't help herself. She knew Pacey was in love with Andie, and she respected it. Kissing him had just been an impetuous expression of her admiration for a guy who could be true to a girl who wouldn't even bend enough to be in a kissing contest with him.

Pacey had wondered later if Courtney would be weird around him when she saw him on the set, but she was fine. In fact, just that day during their lunch break, she'd told him that she was trying to dream up some way for him to talk Andie into entering the kissing contest with him.

Now, how cool was that?

Yes. They had all been so wrong about her back in New York. If he wasn't so totally in love with the one and only McPhee, he would have taken Courtney up on her offer.

As Pacey turned away, Dawson noticed that Joey was massaging Drake's neck.

Courtney brushed her shoulder up against his. "Look at that," she said sourly, her eyes fixed on Joey and Drake. "He couldn't keep his hands off her before. And now it's clear that she feels the same way about him."

"You could be reading motivations that don't exist into an innocent neck rub," Dawson forced himself to say.

"I thought Drake cared about me," Courtney said sadly. "And I thought Joey cared about you. But I guess . . ." The rest of her statement was left hanging.

"Jumping to conclusions is not generally a productive approach to ascertaining the truth," Dawson said. "Their chemistry as Don and Dulcie doesn't necessarily have any bearing at all on the real world."

But Dawson couldn't help it. His eyes skidded over to Joey and Drake again. Now they were laughing with Pacey and Andie, Drake's arm draped casually around Joey's shoulders.

"Why should we lie to ourselves, Dawson?" Courtney breathed in his ear. Her small, soft hand wrapped around his bicep. "After all, they aren't Don and Dulcie now. This is the real world. You're with me, and he's with her."

His eyes met hers.

"Just maybe, Dawson," Courtney said, her voice low and husky, "just maybe this is what's meant to be."

Chapter 10

Pacey carefully led a blindfolded Andie down the stairs to his basement. "Just two more steps," he told her. Outside, thunder rumbled and a driving rain pelted the house.

"What is it with you and blindfolds?" Andie asked as she took the last step. "You blindfolded me when you took me to that bed-and-breakfast, remember? Achoo!" She sneezed loudly.

"Bless you. I enjoy surprising you, McPhee," Pacey said. "It adds a certain dash of romance, don't you think?"

He led her to the center of the room, where he'd laid out a picnic exactly like the one Don and Dulcie shared in Dawson's film. Hearing Andie talk about how romantic the movie was that afternoon, and Courtney talk about trying to help him get Andie to change her mind about the kissing contest, had got him thinking.

Okay. Maybe the love poem/in-line skating thing had been a little over the top. But a romantic picnic should be right up Andie's alley. He wouldn't exactly bring up the contest. There was always the chance that she'd be so blissed out she'd bring it up herself, throw herself into his arms, and tell him she'd be his partner after all.

Hey, a guy could dream.

"Can I look now?" Andie asked.

"*Voilà,*" Pacey said with a flourish as he took the scarf from her eyes.

"Oh, Pacey!" Andie's eyes shone with happiness in the light cast by flickering candles that surrounded the picnic.

"It's just like Don and Dulcie's picnic!" Andie cried.

"Except it's indoors," Pacey pointed out. "The storm interfered with locale."

She knelt down on the blanket, which he'd strewn with rose petals, just like in the movie. There was a picnic basket filled with strawberries and chocolates and a bottle of sparkling cider, and Pacey had borrowed the prop wineglasses.

Pacey sat down with her. "You like it?"

"It's perfect." She leaned over and gave him the softest of kisses. "You're perfect. Thank you."

"No, thank *you,*" Pacey murmured, kissing her again. "Did I mention that only we will be home at Chez Witter this evening?"

"How bilingual of you," Andie said provocatively, leaning in for a kiss. She sneezed again.

Pacey frowned. "You getting a cold, McPhee?

Maybe a basement picnic wasn't such a great idea—"

"It's nothing. I've got some tissues in my purse." She dug around for her little pack of tissues, but instead she came up with a folded piece of paper. "What's this?" She turned it over in her hands.

"Fan mail from some flounder?" Pacey joked.

Andie unfolded it and read it. Her face paled.

"What?" Pacey asked.

She didn't speak, thrusting the piece of paper at him. He read it quickly. *Andie: I saw Pacey kissing Courtney at the beach. —A friend who thinks you should know.*

"Some friend," Pacey said.

"Tell me you were never at the beach with Courtney."

"I can't," Pacey admitted. He saw Andie's face crumple. "But it isn't like that note makes it sound."

"How is it then, Pacey? Did you two kiss?"

God, he wanted to lie to her so badly. But he couldn't. "Yes," he said, his voice low. "But I didn't kiss her. She kissed me."

Andie glared at him, her eyes cold.

"And it didn't mean anything," Pacey rushed on. "We were talking about the kissing contest, and she volunteered to be in it with me, and the next thing I knew she decided to prove she meant it by kissing me."

"But you didn't kiss her back. Or enjoy it. And I'm supposed to believe that," Andie said.

"This is one of those things that sounds so much worse than what actually—"

"Save it," Andie spat. She scrambled to her feet

and looped her purse strap over her shoulder. "Funny how you happened to forget to mention this little episode to me. When did it happen?"

Pacey got up, too. "The night we were out bike riding, after you left. I ran into Jen and Courtney at the ice cream parlor, and . . . I'm telling you, Andie, it was nothing. And I didn't tell you because I knew it would sound like something."

"No, Pacey. You didn't tell me because you didn't want me to know about it. But someone saw the two of you and spilled your little secret. I thought I could trust you!"

"You can!"

Andie's eyes filled with tears. "Maybe Dulcie was right. There really aren't any happily-ever-afters." She turned around, then ran up the stairs and out into the stormy night.

Courtney dropped her overalls on the floor of Jen's bedroom and kicked them into the corner. She peeled off her little T-shirt and heaved it after the overalls. God, to think girls dressed in that ugly crap by *choice!*

She checked out her reflection in the mirror over Jen's dresser and smiled. Perfection. At least she hadn't had to give up her French silk G-strings and matching bras just to look like she fit in here in Hickville. Really, there was only so much she could ask of herself.

She knew Jen was with Dawson in a production meeting, so she had the bedroom to herself. Good. She looked up a phone number in her little address book, punched it into Jen's phone, and plopped down on the bed.

"Chase residence," came a bored female voice.

"Diana? It's me," Courtney said. "God, you sound like a servant. So how goes your au pair job?"

"Can you even believe my witch of a stepmother forced me to work this summer?" Diana said bitterly. "I'm supposed to be 'learning responsibility' because I totaled my new car. Could you vomit?"

"All over," Courtney sympathized. "Is that island off the coast of Maine nice at least?"

"Well, the shopping sucks but the beach is fantastic. There are manly specimens flexing their manly parts all over the place. Mostly all over me," Diana added. "So, are you calling me from . . . what is it, Capetown?"

"You are such an airhead," Courtney laughed. "That's in South Africa. "Jen lives in Capeside. And it is every bit as tacky and agonizing as I knew it would be. Like the town in *October Sky* without the charm of black lung disease. Oh, except for Drake Keller, that hot guy from—"

"*Beacon Bay?*" Diana yelped in Courtney's ear.

"That's him. He's here. Slumming for a month. Every inch of him is mine," Courtney said smugly.

"I'm drooling," Diana said. "So how goes the scam?"

"I am so good I should be illegal," Courtney purred, admiring one raised leg. "I'll fill you in, of course, but it would be a lot easier for you to appreciate my brilliance if you'd actually been at my sweet sixteen and had the joy of meeting them."

"Can I help it if my parents picked the week of your sweet sixteen for a family trip to Belize?"

"I almost forgive you," Courtney said. "Anyway, I have my slut-puppy cousin and her little playmates right where I want them. The two Goober Boys, Dawson and Pacey, both believe I'm hot for them, isn't that a hoot? Jen will forever love Dawson, and he'll forever love Joey, that storky witch Jen brought to my sweet sixteen."

"I heard about her!" Diana exclaimed. "Danny Field told me she did him five minutes after he met her."

"And then the little tramp had the nerve to punch Danny at my sweet sixteen."

"You know, his nose still doesn't look the same," Diana said, "even after my uncle did plastic surgery."

"Well, I have big plans coming up for the stork," Courtney said. "Right now I'm in the process of stealing Dawson from Jen and Joey. It's like taking candy from two babies."

"You're so bad," Diana chuckled.

"This guy Dawson thinks he's a filmmaker, which is a laugh. I was starring in this sucky video he's making. So I pretended to be a really sucky actress to wreck it—"

"But you *are* a really sucky actress," Diana pointed out, puzzled. "Remember that school play where—"

"Kindly shut up," Courtney said. "Where was I? Oh. The other Goober Boy, Pacey," she went on. "I got him to go for a walk on the beach with me, then I pretended to be overcome with passion, and then I stuck my tongue down his throat."

"Yuck."

"Tell me about it," Courtney agreed. "But here's the best part. He is in this boring monogamous thing with this boring girl, Andie. So I slipped a little note into said boring girl's purse, and informed her that an anonymous someone had seen her guy kissing Courtney on the beach and thought she deserved to know. Can you spell 'instant breakup,' boys and girls?"

"Nasty!" Diana squealed.

"Thanks." Courtney stretched out her other leg and frowned. She was due for a waxing. "I predict that by the end of Capeside's tacky little romance festival next weekend, they will not only all hate each other, they'll know the true meaning of public humiliation. Stay tuned."

"Oh, Courtney? I just had the greatest idea!" Diana said. "The Chases are taking their little monsters to grandma's next weekend, so I'm off. Don't you think your dear friend Diana should come visit you?"

"That's a great idea, actually." Courtney sat up. "In fact, you can help me polish off all of them, and we can leave the jerk of Massachusetts far behind. I'll even take Drake with me."

"I'm stoked," Diana said. "So call me later in the week and give me directions and everything, okay?"

Courtney agreed, said good-bye, and hung up.

She put her hands behind her head, and a smile played over her lips.

"You really thought you were going to get away with wrecking my sweet sixteen, didn't you, Jen?" she said aloud. "Well, think again, sweetie. It's payback time."

Chapter 11

Jen ran her fingers through her hair and checked her reflection in the mirror. It was Friday afternoon and she was on her way to the Ice House for the *Don and Dulcie* wrap party. Since Drake had never seen her in anything except pants, she thought it would be fun to dress up a little, so she'd put on a blue camisole and a blue skirt.

She should have been in a great mood. The shooting of the rest of the picture had gone smoothly and quickly. True, it was a simple ten-minute film, nowhere near as complicated as *Creek Daze* to complete, but still, she was proud of it.

Jen felt confident that *Don and Dulcie* would not only be a finalist for the time capsule contest (all three films would be shown at the festival on Sunday), it would win. She had made it happen; she felt good about that. Plus, she really liked Drake.

She knew they'd hang out together tonight, and she had a date with him tomorrow. Lately he had been starring in her steamy dreams instead of Dawson— a good thing.

Unfortunately, there was a dark lining to the silver cloud of her existence. It was—correction, *she* was—at that very moment sitting on her bed.

Diana Hathaway. Jen had known her forever and disliked her for just as long. As a kid, Diana had been lank-haired, skinny, horse-faced, and mean. On top of that, she had the brainpower of a potted geranium. But now, at age sixteen, Diana was a perfectly aerobicized size four with outsized bubble breasts and new and improved facial features, all compliments of her uncle, Dr. Howard Hathaway, plastic surgeon to the stars.

She was still, however, a nasty twit. Diana had always worshipped Courtney, which was why Courtney liked to have her around.

Jen never in a million years thought Diana would ever set foot in her Capeside bedroom. In fact, Jen hadn't been informed of Diana's visit until Diana's Porsche had pulled into Grams' driveway. But here she was all the same, giggling and laughing with Courtney.

"Oh, Jen," Courtney called to her. "I hope you don't mind, but I borrowed that cheap little purse that was in your closet."

"It goes better with the cheap little clothes she's wearing," Diana smirked.

Jen turned to them. "Listen, I hate to interrupt your board meeting, but we need to get a few things straight. Capeside is my home now. If you two do anything to mess up my life here, you will both live to regret it."

"Talk about paranoid," Diana whined.

"I'm sorry you're still insecure about living here," Courtney said. "If this is about that thing with Drake—"

"Just consider yourself warned, both of you."

"Whatever," Diana said dismissively. She went to check out her reflection in the mirror. She had on a white, low-cut, raw-silk crop top, with matching cropped pants. "Do I look fat in this?"

"Like a pig," Jen said, since it was such a ridiculous question. "I'm leaving." She headed for the door.

"Oh, Jen!" Courtney went over to her cousin. "Listen, about Drake. You realize, of course, that he and I are an item, but we've decided to keep it low-key in public."

"Dream on," Jen said.

"I wasn't bragging," Courtney oozed sincerity. "The thing is, everyone's talking about how you've been throwing yourself at Drake. He's kind of embarrassed about it, but he's too nice to say anything. I know you're trying to change your rep, so I was sure you'd want to know."

"Can we just go to the party?" Jen asked them.

"Sure," Courtney said. "I'm glad Dawson told me that Diana could come along."

"Me, too," Diana giggled, and Jen wondered how many more times she'd have to listen to that inane giggle over the next several days. Too many, she was sure.

*   *   *

When they walked into the Ice House, the party was already in full swing. The romance festival wouldn't officially begin until the next day, but the Ice House was already decorated in festival mode. Red helium balloons covered the ceiling, huge hearts that read "Capeside *Is* Romance" adorned the walls, and the tables were covered with pink and red tablecloths.

Even with the party happening, the Ice House was open to the public, and the place was jammed. Bessie had moved the tables around to create a dance floor, and a bunch of people were dancing to music blaring from the jukebox.

Jen immediately separated herself from Courtney and Diana.

Diana looked at the decorations. "Euwww, talk about cheesy!" she yelled over the music. Courtney smiled, but yanked on Diana's silk top so her mouth reached Diana's ear.

"You have a brain the size of a Valium, sweetie," Courtney hissed. "Remember, we *love* Capeside. I spelled the entire plan out for you for a reason, *so follow it.* Got that?"

"I mean, wow, how quaint," Diana amended loudly.

"Much better," Courtney agreed perkily. She led Diana through the crowd, looking for Drake.

"Courtney! Hey, Courtney!"

Pacey edged his way toward them through the gyrating dancers.

"One of the Goober Boys," Courtney whispered to Diana.

"He's kind of cute, though," Diana decided. Courtney gave her a withering look.

"Courtney, hi," Pacey said. "Listen, there's something I really need you to do for me—"

"Do you mind if I introduce you to my friend first?" Courtney interrupted. "Diana Hathaway, Pacey Witter. Pacey, my bud Diana. She's visiting for the weekend."

"Nice to meet you," Pacey said, barely glancing in Diana's direction. "Listen, Courtney, I am in major deep doo-doo with Andie. Some lowlife put a note in Andie's purse saying they saw you and me kissing on the beach."

"Kissing from the neck up or the neck down?" Diana asked.

Pacey stared at her. She appeared to be serious. "Excuse us a minute," he said to her, pulling Courtney a little bit away from Diana.

"The thing is," he continued, "I told Andie what really happened, but she doesn't believe me. So my only shot is if she hears the truth from you. So will you?"

"Pacey, of course!" Courtney assured him.

"Excellent. Come with me." Pacey led Courtney over to Andie, who was sitting at the counter sipping a milk shake.

"The two of you," Andie noted. "Together. Lovely."

"We are not together," Pacey told her. "Courtney came over here to tell you what really happened on the beach."

"I'm all ears," Andie said, her voice flat.

"Well, I asked Pacey to go for a walk with me," Courtney began. "It was perfectly innocent."

"See? Perfectly innocent," Pacey echoed.

"He was telling me how much he wanted to enter the smooch contest so he could win the Viper," Courtney went on, "and he told me you wouldn't enter with him."

"So, in other words, he was hinting that *you* should enter with him," Andie said.

"No," Pacey insisted. "Tell her, Courtney!"

"So I offered to enter with him, just to help him out, and . . . we kissed." Courtney bit her lower lip.

Andie shot a murderous look at Pacey. "Yeah. Real innocent, Pacey."

"It *was* innocent," Pacey insisted. "She kissed me, I didn't kiss her! Courtney, would you tell her?"

"Oh, right," Courtney readily agreed. But as she said it, her eyes slid guiltily over to Pacey. Then she looked away again, as if it was too painful. "We didn't mean to hurt you, Andie. It just . . . happened."

"I would really like to not talk to either one of you, for maybe forever," Andie said, standing up.

"Andie, wait "

Pacey reached for her, but Andie twisted away and took off into the crowd.

Joey set a huge platter of Buffalo wings down on the buffet table so hard that the hot sauce spattered on her shirt.

Perfect. It was bad enough that she was waitressing at the wrap party for a movie she had starred in, but did she also have to be adorned with a disgusting grease stain?

Joey knew it wasn't Bessie's fault that she had to waitress. Bessie had agreed they could have the wrap party at the Ice House on Friday afternoon, and they'd figured that only a handful of tourists would come to town for the festival that was beginning the next day.

Wrong. Who knew tourists for the romance festival would flock to Capeside so early? Who knew they'd flock to Capeside at all? But they had. And the restaurant was beyond packed. Bessie and Jack needed help handling the crowd, so Joey didn't have much choice but to help out.

"Having fun?" Dawson asked, coming over to her.

"Does this look like fun?" She wiped savagely at the large, bloblike stain over her right breast.

"I'd offer to help but I have a feeling you'd say no."

"Very amusing, Dawson." Joey eyed the stain with despair. "Look at me! I'm a walking Rorschach test."

"You look beautiful, actually," Dawson said. "Can I help you, or anything?"

"No. But thanks." Joey gave up on the stain. "I seem to be throwing myself a pity party for one, so ignore me."

"Well, that's just the thing, Joey, I can never ignore you," Dawson said lightly. "I want to tell you again how incredible you are in the film."

A small smile played around her lips. "Yeah?"

"I've got a million ideas for other roles for you."

"I don't think so, Dawson. I mean, I'm flattered that you think I did a good job and didn't wreck your movie, but I'll be sticking to my paints and paper from here on in."

"But why?" Dawson asked.

"Film is your thing, Dawson," Joey said. "Not mine."

"But it can be both our—"

"Joey!" Drake loped over and gave her an exuberant hug. "I'm having a great time. How about you?"

"We were in the middle of a conversation, actually," Dawson pointed out.

"Oh, sorry. Listen. Linda, my agent, was on vacation over in the Berkshires, and she decided to stop here to see me. She's that woman by the jukebox."

"Your Hollywood agent?" Joey asked, wide-eyed.

Drake nodded. "Actually, she's one of my mom's best friends," he admitted, "which is how I lucked out signing with her in the first place. I really want her to meet you, Joey."

Joey laughed. "Yeah, right."

"I'm serious," Drake said. He took Joey's hand. "You don't mind, do you, Dawson? Linda doesn't handle writers or I'd hook you up, too."

"Joey has no interest in acting in films," Dawson said sharply, "so it would be a waste of time."

"I can speak for myself, Dawson," Joey said.

"I'm not taking no for an answer," Drake said good-naturedly. "Come on."

To Dawson's amazement, Joey let Drake lead her away.

Someone who smelled like roses came up behind him and put her hands over his eyes. "Guess who?"

"The perfume says Courtney," Dawson guessed.

"Right on the first try."

Dawson turned, and Courtney kissed him somewhere between his cheek and his lips. Another girl was with her. "I've been looking everywhere for you. I want you to meet my friend Diana. And Diana, this is Dawson, the film genius I was telling you about."

"It's an honor to meet you," Diana said. "Courtney talks about how talented you are all the time. On the phone, I mean."

"That's very nice of her," Dawson said, but he was distracted by the sight, across of the room, of Drake introducing Joey to a tall woman wearing a designer pants suit. He was still holding Joey's hand.

A slow, sexy ballad filled the air. On the dance floor, couples swayed to the music.

"Would you like to dance?" Courtney asked Dawson.

He looked over at Diana. "It's fine with me," Diana assured him. "I'll just see if there's anything on the buffet that isn't a blob of disgusting fried goo."

"The food here is great," Dawson told her. He took Courtney's hand and led her to the dance floor, where she melted into his arms.

"Mmm, perfect fit," she cooed. She put her head on his shoulder, and they danced for a while. "Dawson, could I confide in you about something?"

"Sure."

"It's about Pacey. I thought he was such a terrific guy—I still do, really, but . . ."

"But what?"

"I'm telling you this in total confidence, okay? You know how badly Pacey wants to be in that kissing contest, and you know that Andie turned him down, right?"

Dawson nodded.

"Well, I ran into Pacey the other night," Courtney went on. "I asked him to walk on the beach with me. I know I'm a paranoid New Yorker, but I just didn't feel safe alone."

Dawson nodded again.

"So, he asked me if I'd be in the kissing contest with him. And then . . . then he kissed me."

Dawson pulled back so he could see her. "Pacey kissed you?" he asked incredulously.

Courtney nodded. "But don't be mad at him. He loves Andie. He was just trying to get me to agree to be in the kissing contest with him. The problem is, someone saw us and told Andie. Now she isn't speaking to him."

"Pacey has been known to show a lack of fore-sight that borders on the self-destructive," Dawson allowed.

"Do you think you could talk to Andie and help them get back together? I feel just terrible about it."

"I don't really think there's anything I can do," Dawson said. "What Pacey did is stupid. But Andie knows Pacey loves her. It's really between the two of them."

"I know," Courtney sighed. "But if you could just tell her how much you know Pacey loves her, and that his kissing me was really meaningless."

"I'll try," Dawson conceded.

"I knew I could count on you." Courtney pulled

him close to her again as the song ended, but Dawson let go of her in order to search out Joey in the crowded room.

"Oh look, over there!" Courtney pointed, standing on tiptoe. "Diana's sitting with Drake and Jen and there are two empty seats!"

Diana stood up and waved wildly over her head as Courtney grabbed Dawson's hand and led him to the table.

"I practically had to shoot people to save you two seats," Diana said, taking her purse off one chair and her sweater off the other. "Sit."

When they sat down, Courtney dropped one hand to Dawson's thigh. Jen's eyes flicked to it. "Having fun?" she asked Dawson dryly.

"Sure," he said.

Drake draped his arm around the back of Jen's chair. "Great wrap party."

"Hey, first you're hand in hand with your leading lady, now you're cozying up to the producer, what could be bad?" Dawson asked, his tone biting.

Drake gave him a puzzled look. "What's up with you?"

"Maybe it's PMS," Diana said, giggling. Courtney kicked her under the table.

"I'm sorry," Dawson told Drake. "Forget it."

Diana craned her neck around. "Who do you have to do to get some service here?"

"It's a buffet, remember?" Courtney said.

"There's nothing over there to eat," Diana complained. "I told that woman with the frizzy hair in the kitchen I wanted a salad, and she said fine, someone would bring it to me. But that was, like, a lifetime ago. Then I asked that waiter guy Jack for a Diet Coke and he never brought it."

"I'll get it for you," Dawson offered, rising.

"Oh, wait, here comes the waitress," Diana said.

Joey marched over to their table and set the salad in front of Diana. She couldn't help but notice Courtney's hand draped on Dawson's thigh.

Diana stared into the salad. "*Iceberg* lettuce?"

"Looks like it to me," Joey confirmed. "Dressing?"

"A zillion calories, you must be joking," Diana scoffed.

"Right," Joey agreed. "When I'm not waiting on pleasant customers such as yourself, I do stand-up."

"This is Joey Potter," Dawson said, introducing her to Diana. "Joey's sister owns the restaurant. And Joey had the female lead in *Don and Dulcie*."

"She was awesome," Drake added warmly.

"Joey, this is my dear friend Diana," Courtney said.

"Hi," Joey nodded.

"Do you have balsamic vinegar?" Diana asked her.

"Yep." Joey left to get it.

"So, Drake," Courtney said sweetly, "has Jen told you all about her wild adventures in New York?"

"We were talking about how rank and trashy teen movies have been getting, actually," Drake said.

Jen nodded and took a sip of her Coke. "They're either full of blood and guts, gratuitous T and A, or both."

"And the gratuitous T is always plastic," Drake

went on, "which, personally, I find kind of pathetic."

"Wrong," Diana snapped. "Plastic doesn't droop."

"I'm constantly amazed that Hollywood's concept of female beauty is based on some plastic Barbie fantasy," Dawson said. "It's obvious that the most beautiful and talented women in film don't fit that mold at all."

"I'm with you, bro'," Drake agreed.

"We are sitting with two such highly evolved guys," Courtney said. "It's so refreshing. You can't imagine how shallow guys can be in New York. Don't you think so, Jen?"

"Yeah, a lot of them," Jen agreed.

"Jen's kind of a guy expert," Courtney went on. "I used to just be amazed at how many different guys she could 'date' at once!" She nodded her head almost imperceptibly at Diana, who reached into her purse for something.

"Drop it," Jen muttered.

"You're just being modest," Courtney said. She leaned across the table. "Listen, if there's one thing I admire, it's a girl who turns her life around like you did, Jen. What's that called, when you have sex with pretty much everyone and then you decide not to do it anymore?"

"Second virginity," Diana filled in. She let something fall from her cupped hand into her salad, then quickly pushed a lettuce leaf over it. "So, Jen, did you, like, have to have some kind of surgery for that?"

"Diana, stop it!" Courtney chided her. "We

should be applauding Jen for finally getting some morals."

Jen stood up and pushed her chair so hard that it toppled over. She glared at her cousin and Diana. "You know what? What I did and who I did it with is nobody's business but mine. But I'll tell you this. I would rather be known as the town pump than be known as someone as deliberately cruel as you two."

"What did I say?" Courtney asked, all innocence.

Drake stood, too. "Jen—"

"Oh, my God!" Diana shrieked at the top of her lungs, just as Joey returned with the vinegar. "There's a spider in my salad!"

"There can't be," Joey said, hurrying over to her.

"A *spider?*" Courtney gasped.

All around them, heads turned.

"Euwww! There's a spider in my salad!" Diana yelled even louder. "My salad is *infested!*" She forked out the spider and threw it on the floor, then stomped on it as she screamed her head off.

"It's just one little spider," Joey insisted, her cheeks burning with embarrassment.

"What?" a woman at the next table, obviously a tourist, asked her husband.

"She found a spider in her food," the man replied with disgust. "Miss!" he called to Joey. "Cancel our food order." They got up and walked out.

Word spread through the Ice House. Though Joey, Jen, and Dawson tried to stop them, a half-dozen other tourists also left.

"Get the stupid spider," Jen hissed at Dawson.

133

Then she went from table to table, calming people down.

But Courtney had already scooped up the crushed spider in her napkin.

"I'll get rid of this for you, Joey." Courtney hurried away with the napkin.

"I think I'm going to puke," Diana groaned, running after Courtney.

She and Courtney met up a few hundred feet from the Ice House. Both of them laughed hysterically.

"That was perfect," Courtney squealed, between peals of laughter. She opened the napkin. "And here's our lovely little rubber spider, compliments of the rubber bug collection of my new best friend in the under-twelve category, Dina Wolfe." She dropped the rubber spider into her purse.

"That was more fun than a bottle of champagne," Diana said, giggling.

Courtney flashed an evil smile. "And we aren't done yet, Diana. Not by a long shot."

Chapter 12

Jen paced back and forth in front of the in-line skate rental stand in the park. She checked her watch again. It was five minutes after ten. Where were they?

When she'd gotten back to Grams' after the wrap party fiasco, Courtney and Diana were nowhere to be seen. Good. Jen had picked up the phone and called Dawson, Joey, Pacey, and Andie, and told them all to meet her by the in-line skate stand at ten o'clock. She said it was about the movie and it was urgent. No, she'd said, they could not meet at Grams' house. Not under any circumstances.

What if they'd all blown her off?

"Interesting locale for a production meeting," Pacey said, ambling over from the parking lot, Joey beside him. "I borrowed my father's sacred truck, so I hope whatever this is about is short and sweet."

"This shouldn't take long," Jen assured him.

"So, where's your cousin and her artificially augmented little friend?" Pacey asked.

"Don't know, don't care."

Dawson walked up with Andie, who stood as far from Pacey as possible, refusing to make eye contact with him.

"What is this about, Jen?" Dawson asked. "I still have at least two hours of editing left on the film. It has to be turned in to the judges by nine tomorrow morning."

"It's about what's going on with us," Jen said. "I hate it, and I'm guessing that all of you hate it, too."

"Nothing is going on," Joey said.

"Right," Jen agreed. "That's my point. We're supposed to be friends. Working on Dawson's movie was supposed to be fun. Instead, we're all barely speaking to each other."

"If you called us together for some kind of quasi-group therapy moment, I think I've heard enough," Joey opined.

"I'm with you," Pacey agreed. "The sacred truck awaiteth." He and Joey started to walk toward the parking lot.

"Hold it, you two," Andie said sharply. "Walking away isn't going to solve anything, you know."

Pacey turned to her. "Neither is your not trusting me."

"How am I supposed to trust you, Pacey? You asked Courtney to tell me the truth, she told me the truth. Which makes you guilty as charged."

"Andie," Jen said, "Courtney wouldn't know the truth if it jumped up and bit her butt."

"I know you and Courtney have had your differences in the past, Jen," Dawson said. "But from what I can see, she's changed. I mean, she worked on the film even after losing the role to Joey. That was incredibly nice of her."

"So nice she keeps her hand superglued to your thigh," Joey muttered.

"It seems to me you were the one who was hand in hand with the soap-stud at the wrap party," Dawson reminded her.

"He was introducing me to his agent!" Joey exclaimed.

"Right after you told me that you had no interest in acting in any more films," Dawson pointed out. "Or did that just apply to *my* films? At least Courtney shows a little enthusiasm for my work."

"Enthusiasm for *you*, maybe," Joey shot back.

"No, no," Andie said. "It's not Dawson who Courtney has her eye on." She turned to Pacey. "Or should I say, her *lips* on."

"Once more with feeling: *she* kissed *me*," Pacey said. "You either believe me, or you don't."

"Don't," Andie snapped.

"Fine," Pacey replied. "If that's your idea of love—"

Dawson looked at Pacey. "Are you denying that you deliberately kissed Courtney to manipulate her into—"

"What is this, the Capeside Premillennial Inquisition?" Pacey exploded.

"Courtney is upset that you used her," Dawson said. "She kissed me as part of her Dulcie character, which is discernibly different from you kissing her just to—"

"You both kissed Courtney?" Andie asked incredulously.

"Who cares about Courtney?" Joey yelled. "Oh, wait, that's right, you do, Dawson."

Andie shot Pacey a murderous look. "Well. Maybe you and Dawson can take turns."

Everyone began arguing at once, talking over each other. Finally, Jen gave a piercing whistle through her fingers. Startled, they fell silent.

"Do you hear us?" Jen asked. "We sound like a bunch of kindergarteners. Don't you see what she's doing to us?"

They all looked at each other uneasily.

"And I know why," Jen went on. "Drake said to me, 'Jen, your cousin is the most manipulative person I've ever met. And coming from an L.A. actor, that's saying a lot.' So I thought about how Courtney came on to Dawson *and* to Pacey."

"But—" Joey began.

"Joey," Jen went on, "I bet she and Diana cooked up that spider incident just to embarrass you. For God's sake, she must be telling everyone in Capeside that I'm a—a slut, because I'm hearing that word from everybody. Don't you get it? She played us! My insecurities, Joey's pride, and Dawson's and Pacey's egos. It's payback for her sweet sixteen. *She set us up.*"

For a long time, there was silence. Finally, it was Andie who spoke.

"Okay, I know I am the only person present who was not at this infamous sweet sixteen party," Andie said. "But it seems to me that Courtney hurt me because that would hurt Pacey." She looked at Pacey. "I believe Jen. And you. I was wrong. I apologize."

Pacey smiled at her. "I always said you had brains, McPhee." He hugged her.

"I think you're right, too," Joey reluctantly told Jen. "I'm just amazed that we all fell for it."

Jen cocked her head at Dawson. "Well?"

"It's hard to accept that anyone who seems so nice could actually be so deliberately cruel," he said.

"Welcome to the real world, Dawson," Jen said. She reached into her pocket and took out a rubber spider. "Look familiar? I found it in the purse Courtney borrowed from me. Sorry to burst your bubble, but cruelty is Courtney's middle name."

"That chick played us like a violin," Pacey said, holding Andie close.

"The question now is, what do we do about it?" Joey asked.

"I have an idea," Jen said.

Everyone turned to her.

"In the words of those cliché-ridden old Westerns, this town ain't big enough for both of us. So I say we kick her out of Dodge."

Jen took the steps up to her room two at a time. Courtney was sitting cross-legged in the middle of her bed wearing Jen's robe, giving herself a pedicure.

"Honestly, doing this yourself is slave labor," Courtney groused, dabbing pale pink polish on her toenails.

"Watch it, Courtney, your halo is falling. Where's Diana?"

"She went to some party in Boston with that guy Chris Wolfe," She smiled at Jen. "I understand he's one of your many exes. I hope it doesn't break your heart that he's with her."

"I'll mend," Jen said dryly. "Listen, can you come downstairs with me? There's something I want to show you."

"Can't it wait? I'll wreck my pedicure."

"Walk on your heels," Jen suggested.

Courtney sighed dramatically and carefully scuttled to the door. The she followed Jen downstairs.

"Well?"

"It's out in front," Jen explained.

Courtney sighed again, tightened the sash on Jen's robe, and followed Jen outside.

Joey, Pacey, Andie, and Dawson were waiting for her. They didn't look happy.

"Hi!" Courtney said brightly. "If we're having a party, you guys have to let me go get dressed."

"I guess you could look at it as a party," Joey said. "In your honor."

"Awww, you guys." Courtney put her hands over her heart.

"In honor of you getting your butt out of Capeside, that is," Andie added.

Courtney looked around uncertainly. "This is a joke, right?"

"Notice how many of us are laughing," Jen said.

"But . . . we're friends."

"I'll say this much for you, Courtney," Pacey said. "You're a much better actress than we gave you credit for. I must confess you had me going there for a while. But then I've always been a slow learner."

Courtney shook her head, bewildered. "I don't know what you're all talking about."

Jen dangled the plastic spider in Courtney's face.

"What?" Courtney asked. Then she gasped. "Are you telling me that Diana pulled some kind of a prank at the Ice House with a plastic spider?"

"Nice try," Joey said.

"You have until ten o'clock tomorrow morning, when the festival starts, to disappear," Jen told her.

"If you're not out of Capeside by then," Joey went on, "we will do something to you that makes what you did to us look like kiddie play."

"To reiterate, you are gone by ten," Jen concluded.

Courtney looked at all of them. Then she slowly walked over to Dawson. She stared up at him, her eyes luminous. "Dawson? You don't believe those lies about me, do you?"

He gazed at her for a moment, and Courtney thought she saw him wavering. She put her hand on his arm.

"Courtney, let's make that nine fifty-five," Dawson said.

Jen punched her pillow into a new position and squinted at the numerals of her digital clock. It was two-thirty in the morning. Courtney had gotten dressed right after their showdown and peeled off in her Saab. As for Diana, she wasn't back yet from her date with Chris, but her car was still in the driveway. Jen was sure Courtney would be back sometime, because she'd neglected to take all her stuff.

Jen must have dozed off, because she was startled awake by the sound of a crash. She turned on the light. An obviously wrecked Courtney lay on the floor.

"I tripped over someone's friggin' shoe in the middle of the friggin' floor," Courtney slurred. "Oh. Mine." She laughed hysterically.

"You're toasted," Courtney observed.

"Well, aren't you the rocket scientist? Could you help me up, or would that contaminate your new-found purity?"

"You can sleep right there for all I care. I'll be sure to wake you in time to pack up in the morning." Jen clicked out the light and turned over.

The room was silent. Jen closed her eyes, determined to go back to sleep, as Courtney began to cry quietly.

"Jen?" she whispered.

Jen ignored her.

"Look, I know you hate me," Courtney went on. "I don't blame you. I pretty much hate myself. You were right about everything, okay? I know it's too much to ask but . . . can you ever forgive me?" Sobs filled the night air.

Jen turned the light back on. Courtney was sitting cross-legged on the rug, black mascara tracking down her cheeks.

"Why should I?" Jen asked. "Because you asked? Because you're crying? Both are utterly meaningless."

"It's just that . . . just that . . . there's so much

you don't understand," Courtney gasped out through her tears.

Jen reached for the box of tissues on her nightstand and pitched it at Courtney.

"Thanks." Courtney blew her nose loudly. "I was never much for baring my soul. But there's something I want to tell you, Cuz."

"Save it—"

"No, I *have* to tell you," Courtney insisted. "You don't have to listen, but I have to say it. You know my perfect parents? The ones who threw themselves that two-hundred-thousand-dollar twentieth-anniversary party that was in the Sunday *New York Times?* Well, big joke. They're getting divorced. It seems daddy dearest has been doing the nasty with the bimbo who used to baby-sit for me—how's that for a cliché? And ever since my mother found out, she's been spiking her own orange juice for breakfast. She's a total wreck."

"So that gave you license to come here and try to wreck my life?" Jen asked.

"No." Courtney blew her nose again. "It's funny. You're the first person I've told. You'd think I'd tell one of my so-called *dear* friends," she said bitterly, "Amy or Alexis, or even Diana—but I haven't. The truth is, none of them would care. If it's not about shopping or partying or who's doing what to who, they are monumentally bored. They don't really give a rat's behind about me."

"What do you expect?" Jen asked. "You get back what you give out."

"I know." Courtney shredded a tissue between her fingers. "The reason I keep ragging on you for changing your life is because I haven't been able to change mine. So I wanted to do something really ugly to you out of stupid jealousy. I admit it."

"Am I supposed to care?" Jen asked.

"No. But not having anyone really care about you feels so lonely, Jen. I guess I thought . . . I *hoped* that deep down you might. Not because you have to. Or even want to. But because we're family. We're all the family we've got."

"Wait. You expect me to buy this?"

"Never mind." Courtney stumbled to her feet. "I'll pack up and leave now. I know you don't want me around."

"You can't drive, you're wrecked." Jen thought a minute. "Do my parents know?"

"Your mom is lording it over my mom, which is payback for all the years my mom lorded it over your mom." Courtney pulled her T-shirt over her head. It got stuck.

Jen got up and pulled Courtney's T-shirt all the way off. "You can't let your parents' problems wreck your life, Courtney. I learned that the hard way. You're the one who suffers, so what's the point?"

"Yeah," Courtney agreed. She stumbled out of her jeans, and weaved her way to her bed. "I really want to make up for what I did. Maybe I could write all your friends a letter of apology."

Jen lifted Courtney's legs and pulled off her sandals. An idea began to form in her mind. "If you really want to apologize, I have a better idea."

"What?" Courtney asked.

"Show up at the bandstand tomorrow morning at

ten o'clock. I'll make sure all my friends are there. Everyone else in Capeside will be there, too, because it's the opening ceremonies for the romance festival."

Courtney managed to lift her head. "That's it?"

"No, that's not it. This is. You use the microphone on the bandstand to make a public apology to everyone you scammed. Name names. You'll also tell how you and Diana planted a rubber spider in the salad at the Ice House and beg Joey and Bessie to forgive you."

"Why don't you just stick a scarlet *A* on my chest and call me Demi Moore?" Courtney groaned.

"This is not a bad film, Courtney. This is real life. *My* life. I have real friends here who care about me and respect me. And I earned it. So don't go asking me to feel sorry for you because your too rich, too shallow parents are doing what too rich, too shallow people do. My parents wrote the novel; your parents' tawdry little drama is just a short story in comparison. If you want to skip the apologies and leave without owning up to what you did, it's fine with me. You'll just be carrying on the family tradition. Just don't ask me to care."

Tears slid down Courtney's face and dripped silently onto the sheet. "I don't want to be like them, Jen. I swear I don't." She fisted the tears away. "I'll do it."

Chapter 13

"Hello, welcome to the Capeside Romance Festival. Would you like a button?" Andie asked, over and over, as she worked her way through the sizable crowd surrounding the bandstand.

It was close to ten o'clock in the morning, official kickoff time for the festival, and already Andie and the other official hosts and hostesses had given away hundreds of "Capeside *Is* Romance" buttons. Many of the tourists had also purchased the official white-with-red-letters festival T-shirt.

Even from where Andie stood, she could see the beaming faces of the city council members, the mayor, and Pacey's policeman dad, who were all seated up on the bandstand. The Capeside Romance Festival, hastily put together and with limited funds for advertising, was a resounding success.

"Hello, welcome to the Capeside Romance Festi-

val. Would you like a button?" Andie asked a di-
minutive elderly couple who were looking through
the schedule of activities. Neither was much more
than five feet tall, and both were already clad in
festival T-shirts.

"Well, bless your heart . . . Andie," the tiny, plump
woman said, peering at Andie's official hostess name
tag. "I'm Florence Shervin, and this is my husband,
Mervin Shervin. Please call us Flo and Merv."

"Nice to meet you, Flo and Merv," Andie said.
"Where are you from?"

"Eh?" her husband asked, pointing to his ear.

"He's a little hard of hearing," Flo explained.

"I asked where you were from," Andie said loudly.

"Oh. Dalton, Mass," Mervin boomed. "Ever
been?"

"Can't say that I have," Andie said politely.

"Eh?"

"NO!" Andie yelled.

Flo put her hand on Andie's arm. "You know, we
were surfing the Net, and that's where we read
about this festival. I said to Merv, 'Gracious, dear,
that's for us.' And can you guess why?"

"You're . . . romantic?" Andie ventured.

"Fifty years," Flo said, smiling. "Tomorrow is our
fiftieth wedding anniversary."

"Eh?" Merv asked.

"FIFTY YEARS!" Flo repeated.

"You ain't just whistlin' Dixie," Merv agreed.
"Best thing I ever did."

"That's so beautiful!" Andie exclaimed. "I wish
my boyfriend could meet you."

"Eh?"

"SHE WANTS US TO MEET HER BOY-FRIEND!" Flo yelled.

"Abso-tively, love to, bring him on," Merv boomed.

"Well, he's supposed to meet me here," Andie said, "so when I find him I'll come and find you. Okay?"

"Eh?"

"I SAID—"

"That's all right, Andie dear," Flo assured her. "You can run along and I'll pass that on to Merv."

Andie continued to work her way toward the bandstand, where she was supposed to meet her friends. Jen had called her early that morning to say that Courtney had had some kind of change of heart, and at ten sharp, she'd be making a public apology over the PA at the bandstand, and it was imperative that they all be there.

When Andie finally reached the side steps of the bandstand, Dawson, Pacey, and Joey had already arrived. And they did not look happy.

"You three are not the most romantic-looking people at this romance festival," Andie observed. "Where's Jen?"

"Good question," Dawson said. "One of the hosts just delivered this phone message to us." He handed Andie a pink phone message slip.

"Dawson, Pacey, Joey, and Andie," she read aloud. "Can't meet you. Courtney will show up at ten to apologize. She promised. —Jen." Andie looked up. "Suddenly Jen believes Courtney's promises?"

"I left Bessie with a restaurant full of hungry tourists just so I could hear this alleged apology," Joey said. "And it isn't important enough for Jen to be here."

"Or Courtney, for that matter, it looks like," Pacey said, checking his watch. "It's five after ten. And once the mayor starts the festivities, forget it. My dad's speech alone could take the better part of the day."

"Well, I'm beat," Dawson said, yawning. "I was up until four finishing the edits on *Don and Dulcie*. And Jen called me at six forty-five."

"When we find Jen, we can all vent," Joey said. "Meanwhile, it's pretty apparent that Courtney is not gonna show. Big duh there. I gotta get back to the Ice—"

"Yoo-hoo! Dawson! Pacey!" Diana pushed her way through the crowd toward them. She wore Ralph Lauren, head to toe, and hid her eyes behind oversized white sunglasses.

"I'm so glad I caught you!" Diana said breathlessly.

"Gee, us, too," Joey deadpanned.

"Courtney has some kind of icky stomach thing," Diana explained. "She feels terrible about not being here to apologize, after she promised. So she asked me to come do it for her. I said yes."

"And when, might I ask, will you two be riding your broomsticks out of town?" Andie asked.

"Oh, that's a joke, right?" Diana asked.

"Not really," Andie replied coolly.

"I knew that. We're leaving right after this," Diana said. "Courtney says we should leave you in peace."

"Or did she mean *pieces*," Joey asked.

"Okay, so she messed up," Diana said. "Cut her a little slack. Haven't you ever messed up?"

"Yeah," Joey admitted. "I have."

"Okay, well . . ." Diana pulled a small piece of folded paper out of her pocket. "I'm nervous, but I'm ready."

"How do we pull this off, exactly?" Joey asked, looking over at the town leaders sitting on the bandstand.

"I'll handle it," Pacey decided.

As the others watched, Pacey went to talk with his father on the bandstand. Then his father talked to the mayor, then the mayor smiled, nodded yes, and shook hands with Pacey while Pacey's dad clapped him on the back.

"Amazing," Dawson observed. "Short of telling them that Capeside has been selected as the site for the next Olympic Games, what could Pacey possibly have said to elicit that kind of a reaction?"

Pacey skipped back down the steps. "Okay, Diana. You're on."

"Pacey, what did you tell them?" Andie asked.

Pacey put an arm around Diana's bony shoulders. "It's like this, Diana. I told them that you were filthy rich, and you were so impressed with Capeside that you've decided to make a major donation to the Widows and Orphans Fund of the Capeside Police Auxiliary. And you are, right?"

"Yeah, if they take Visa," Diana said vaguely.

"And be sure to mention that in your speech," Pacey said. "Or I will have no choice but to kill you, right before my father kills me."

Diana stepped up onto the bandstand, where all the dignitaries shook her hand. Then she went to the microphone. "Testing, one, two, three," she said, her voice booming out over the crowd. "Oh, wow. This is loud!"

The crowd hushed.

"Uh, hi." Now she read directly from her paper. "My name is Diana Hathaway. I live in New York City. I was very excited to come to Capeside because I had heard what a beautiful place this is with all the nature, and also beautiful people, too."

"Guess whose future does not include the word 'writer'?" Pacey whispered to Andie.

"My friend and I have had a very nice time here in Capeside. But I am distressed to have to tell you about one negative experience that has psychologically scarred me and my friend. Yesterday we ate at a restaurant called the Ice House. While dining there I found a live spider crawling through my salad."

"I'm dead," Pacey said.

"No, *she's* dead," Joey seethed.

Behind her on the bandstand, the town leaders all looked as if they had just swallowed the spider Diana was talking about.

"Finding a live spider in my food made me feel sick," Diana went on. "I felt it was only fair to let all of you know about this terrible experience at the Ice House. But other than that, Capeside is a very nice place."

She turned from the mike, and then stepped back to it quickly. "Oh, one last thing," Diana squeaked. "I am making a donation to the Widows and Orphans of the Cops Fund. Or whatever." Before Pacey could move, she fled from the stage in the opposite direction, losing herself in the crowd.

Red-faced with embarrassment, the mayor went to begin his welcoming speech.

Sheriff Witter, his face showing his fury, bounded off the platform and hurried to his son. "Of all the—"

"Can't chat now, Dad, gotta run." Pacey and his friends pushed through the crowd in an effort to pursue Diana.

"We can take my dad's truck to Jen's," Pacey said. "She'll be going back there to meet Courtney, I bet. And I for one would like to know exactly what is going on here."

"What does it look like is going on?" Joey fumed. "Who do you think Courtney holds responsible for wrecking her precious sweet sixteen party? Who was it who punched her friend Danny in the nose somewhere in the vicinity of that tasteful, life-size, Courtney-shaped ice sculpture? Me."

"I thought Danny's blood added a certain dashing reality to the ice sculpture, myself," Pacey mused, as they jogged along toward the truck.

"I can't believe Diana just did what she did," Andie said. "We must be the four most gullible people in history."

"I'm telling you, something about this isn't making sense," Dawson insisted, as they reached the truck and piled into it. "Jen must have seriously believed that Courtney was going to show up and apologize."

Joey looked sideways at him. "Dawson, at the risk

of toppling the pedestal on which you have delusionally placed Jen, please notice who besides Courtney didn't show up."

As Pacey started the truck and pulled out of the parking lot, Dawson responded, "Jen has nothing to do with what just happened. And I don't put her on a pedestal, Joey."

"No?" Joey asked. "Who now produces all your movies? Who can you talk to when you can't talk to me because with me it's just too complicated as to what we are and how we are? Jen, who is so much more sophisticated than me and so much more—"

"I'm not going to let you make this about her, Joey!"

Andie leaned forward. "You guys, can we just—"

"You're not going to *let* me?" Joey exploded.

"It's getting mighty hot in here," Pacey observed.

"Look, I understand that you're hurt over what Diana just did," Dawson glanced at Joey. "But you can't make it be about Jen when it isn't."

"Let me put it to you this way," Joey said. "On Planet Dawson, where idealism and happily-ever-afters are known throughout the kingdom, Jen would never turn on us. But here on Planet Capeside, where Jen loved and lost, and holds both of us responsible for it, maybe she would."

"You're wrong. I know Jen," Dawson said as Pacey turned down the short road leading to Dawson's and Jen's houses. He looked at Joey, Pacey, and Andie. "And so do all of you."

Chapter 14

Pacey pulled the truck up in front of Jen's house. Courtney's Saab was gone. And so was Diana's Porsche.

"Well, we told 'em to leave," he said dryly.

"Unbelievable." Andie shook her head. "They got away with it. I *hate* that."

"You don't really believe that Jen took off with them, do you?" Pacey asked Joey.

"Right now, I'd believe just about anything."

Dawson got out of the truck and walked resolutely to Jen's front door, the others trailing behind him. He knocked hard. Grams appeared.

"Well, how fortuitous," she said. "I was just on my way over to the festival to try and locate you people. Jennifer just called. She said it's urgent that you all meet her at Eve Keller's house—she's Drake

154

Keller's aunt." Grams handed Dawson a slip of paper with the address on it.

"I know where it is," Dawson said.

"What is up with Jen?" Pacey asked, turning his palms up in frustration. "The mysterious phone call thing is getting a little tired here."

"I'm sure I have no idea," Grams said. "But I know this much about my granddaughter. If Jennifer says it's urgent, it is."

"Thanks," Dawson said. "We appreciate it."

"You're entirely welcome," Grams replied. "You know, Dawson, when you aren't sneaking into my home through Jennifer's window, you're a very nice young man." She closed the door.

Dawson looked at his friends. "Let's go."

No one moved.

"I have to get back to the festival, Dawson," Andie said. "I'm supposed to be a meet-and-greet hostess, remember? They're *paying* me?"

"And I have to get back to the Ice House and see how much damage Diana's little speech did," Joey said.

"I'll come with you," Pacey said. "Right now anywhere far from Sheriff Witter is where I want to be."

"We all go or none of us go," Dawson insisted.

Joey sucked in her cheeks with annoyance. "Are you adding 'king of the world' to your list of credits, Dawson?"

"All I'm trying to do is—"

"Time out, you two," Andie said. "Look, if for some bizarre reason Jen is in on some scam with her New York friends, then fine," Andie said. "If she isn't, that's fine, too. I have enough drama in my life, thank you very much. I just don't care about all this anymore."

"I'll second that," Joey said.

"And I'm the amen corner," Pacey added.

"Well, I care," Dawson said. "Look, Jen isn't perfect. And while I clearly misjudged Courtney, I don't think I've misjudged Jen. You used to fault me for putting *you* on a pedestal. I took you down, Joey. You're not perfect. Neither is Pacey, or Andie, or me. Or Jen, for that matter. Don't you realize that sometimes she still feels like an outsider in Capeside? Even now? And I just don't know how much we've all done to help her get over that feeling. She's our friend. And whatever the truth is, I'm not going to stop believing in her just because she isn't perfect, any more than I'd stop believing in you."

One corner of Joey's mouth tugged up in a smile. "Nice speech. Very eleventh-hour-rally-the-troops and all that."

"Most big stars insist on them at the end of their movies nowadays," Pacey observed. "Yours could do with some editing, Dawson."

"You did get a little too Sidney Poitier *To Sir, with Love*–ish," Andie agreed as they all headed back to the truck. "Did you ever hear the title song? My mom used to sing it while she was gardening. How did it go?"

"I was thinking more *Knute Rockne—All American*," Pacey mused. "You know, win-this-one-for-the-Gipper."

"The Gipper in the movie being former President Reagan," he reminded them.

"Oh, I remember! 'Those school-girl days . . .'" Andie warbled.

Drake's aunt's house was only five minutes away. When they got there, Courtney's pale pink Saab was parked in the driveway. "Now I am totally confused," Andie said, as Pacey pulled up.

Jen was sitting in Courtney's car, waiting for them. She got out, hurried over, opened the back door, and squished in with Pacey and Andie.

"Hello," Pacey said, giving Jen a quizzical look.

"You guys made it," Jen said happily.

"Jen, you know those dot-to-dot books you used to do when you were a kid?" Pacey asked. "Where you connect all the dots to see the picture? Well, we connected the dots here, and it still looks amazingly like bad modern art."

"In other words," Andie said, "what is going on?"

"Okay, here's the *Cliff Notes* version, because time is of the essence," Jen said. "Last night Courtney gave me a sob story about how her unhappy home life made her so jealous of our friendship that she wanted to hurt me and all of you. Her performance deserved an Academy Award, meaning I almost believed her. So I decided I'd give her one last chance to apologize to everyone, which would be the least she could do—"

"But she didn't show up this morning," Andie said. "Diana did. She made a speech about finding a live spider in her salad at the Ice House."

"Yeah, I know," Jen said.

"You *know*?" Joey repeated.

157

"Do you really think that when it comes to the Cousin from Hell, I'm not gonna cover my butt?"

Andie pressed her fingertips to her temples. "I'm more confused than ever here."

"Let me cut to the chase. Diana spent the night with Chris Wolfe, Courtney called her there this morning. I listened in on the call and heard them planning their final scam. And that's when I planned *my* counterscam."

"Meaning?" Andie asked, bewildered.

"Say Courtney's the fish," Jen explained. "Drake is the bait. He called her, said she was the woman for him, he had to be with her, yada-yada-yada. And the fish bit—hook, line, and sinker."

"Because Drake is into you and she's jealous?" Andie guessed.

Jen grinned. "Courtney would never turn down the opportunity to both steal a guy away from me and show off a soap opera hunk to her friends in New York. Right now Drake is telling her that he can't bear to let her leave, so how about if he goes back to New York with her? The sound you hear, boys and girls, is the fish flopping on the end of my line."

"You're good," Andie said with admiration.

"I know." Jen checked her watch. "They should be ready to make their big romantic getaway just about—"

The front door opened and Drake and Courtney came out of the house. Drake took her in his arms.

"—now," Jen said smugly.

"So what happens next?" Andie asked, fascinated.

"Next, we enter this little ESPN fishing show," Jen said, opening the car door. "Remember, you don't know a thing. I suggest you go for devastated-but-resigned."

Courtney saw them over Drake's shoulder. "Well, what are the losers and misfits of Capeside doing here?"

"Drake called me," Jen said solemnly. "He said you were the only woman for him. I just couldn't believe it, frankly. I wanted to hear him say it to my face." She glanced at her friends. "I asked them to come with me for moral support."

Courtney smiled. "How nauseating." She snaked her arm around Drake. "Drake's coming to New York with me. I told you, Jen. When it comes to guys, you are *so* no comp."

"Sorry, Jen," Drake said.

With their arms around each other's waists, Drake and Courtney walked to her car. Courtney turned back to them. "Well, as my friend Dina Wolfe would say, 'It was real. And it was fun. But it wasn't real fun.' "

"Okay, you got back at us for your sweet sixteen," Joey acknowledged.

"And we're devastated," Andie said. "But resigned."

Pacey went up to Courtney. "I . . . I really thought you and I had something going." His voice choked with emotion.

Courtney threw her head back and laughed. "Please! Take a look at you. Now take a look at Drake. Need I say more?" She raised her lips for a kiss from Drake.

Drake pulled away. "Oh, man, Courtney, your breath *stinks!*" He waved a hand in front of his face, brushing the air away.

"What?" Courtney cried.

"And there's this body-odor thing you got goin' on," he continued. He turned to them. "The girl sweats like a pig. Courtney, haven't you ever heard of personal hygiene?"

Courtney's cheeks blazed red. "What are you *talking* about?"

"Then there's the farting," Drake continued. "You think that just because I can't hear 'em, I can't smell 'em? Don't you have any respect for yourself?"

Courtney looked so incensed that Andie couldn't help it. A snorting laugh escaped through her nose. That made everyone else laugh, and then no one could stop.

"Oh, you think this is so funny?" Courtney snapped.

"Yes, actually," Drake said. "And you *do* stink, Courtney. As a human being."

"You . . . you bastard," Courtney seethed. She hauled off to slap him, but he caught her wrist.

"You're right, I didn't play nice," Drake acknowledged, "but not nearly as not-nice as you deserve. And just for the record, when it comes to Jen, you are *so* no comp."

"And that, ladies and gentlemen, is the happy ending to *Jaws XI: The Return of Courtney,*" Jen said, bowing.

Drake opened the car door for Courtney. "Bye, Courtney. Have a nice life."

"Or as our friend Dina Wolfe would say," Jen added, " 'See ya, wouldn't want to be ya.' "

"Bye! Bye-bye!" Pacey and Andie called, in their best, high-pitched Munchkin voices.

"I loathe and despise every single one of you." Courtney got in the car and slammed the door shut.

Joey leaned in her window. "Before you go, there's something I really would like to understand, Courtney. Okay, Pacey and Dawson crashed your party in New York, but they didn't do it to hurt you. And I punched your friend Danny in the nose. But he was telling malicious lies about me and he more than deserved it. The fact is, none of us, including Jen, really did anything to hurt you. And yet you got some perverse pleasure in coming here to hurt us. And I'd really like to know why."

Courtney stared straight ahead. They all waited silently, to hear what she would say. Slowly, she turned her head, but instead of looking at Joey, she looked past her. At Jen.

"If you think this is over," Courtney began, "you are sadly mistaken. As for Drake, he's probably a closet case."

"Enjoy your boring little lives in your boring little town," Courtney went on. "And Dawson, your movie sucks." She started the car, pushed the button to roll up her window, and peeled out of the driveway.

Dawson watched her car disappear down the street. "How could I have been so wrong about her?"

"Because, as I keep telling you," Joey said, "you are a hopeless romantic who always believes the good about people before he believes the bad. It happens to be a very rare and very lovely thing," she added grudgingly.

"What we all just did is extremely juvenile," Andie observed. "And empty and futile and senseless."

"Yeah," Pacey agreed, putting his arms around her. "Wasn't it great?"

"Thanks, Drake," Jen told him. "I mean it."

He grinned. "In some perverse way, it was my pleasure."

"Well, revenge is sweet and all that," Joey said, "but I have to get back to the Ice House and do some damage control about the spider thing. Although I don't have a clue how."

"This might help." Drake pulled a letter out of his back pocket.

"What is it?" Joey asked.

"It was Jen's idea," Drake said. "I told Courtney that before we ran off together, there were a couple of things I wanted her to do. Like leave behind a notarized letter admitting that the spider in the salad was rubber and was meant as a practical joke."

Pacey was incredulous. "She actually did it?"

"Besides the fact that Courtney wanted badly to steal Drake away from me and dangle him in front of her friends," Jen explained, "Drake insisted to her that he couldn't leave with her unless she made things right for Bessie's sake. After all, Bessie didn't crash her sweet sixteen party!"

"And my aunt is a notary public, which made it

easy," Drake added, handing the letter to Joey. "Oh, Pacey, there's a check in there, too."

"Thanks, man," Pacey said.

"Check for what?" Dawson asked.

"Widows and Orphans Fund, Capeside Police Auxiliary," Pacey said.

"That's the other thing I asked Courtney to do," Drake said. "To show Capeside what a beautiful person she is."

"What?" Pacey asked. "You thought I came up with that on the spur of the moment? Much as I'd like to take credit, Jen suggested it when she called me this morning. Although I have to tell you, Jen, after Diana showed instead of Courtney and pulled her stunt, I was starting to worry."

Dawson looked at Jen with admiration. "You are amazing, do you know that?"

Jen couldn't help smiling. "Glad you think so," she said shyly.

Joey tapped the letter against her hand. "Thank you for this, Jen, really."

"You're welcome."

Joey's eyes slid over to Dawson, then back to Jen. "Sometimes I . . . I still seem to fall into a very bad habit I have of not appreciating what a good person you are. And I apologize for that."

"Accepted," Jen said quietly.

"Oh, my gosh!" Andie yelped. "Look at the time. I've got to get back to the festival immediately!"

"The hostess with the mostest, huh?" Pacey quipped.

"Forget that," Andie scoffed. "I'm turning in my red T-shirt—figuratively speaking, of course. Pacey

Witter, don't you realize that the kissing contest starts in ten minutes?"

Pacey's face broke into a long, slow grin. "You mean?"

"Pacey, I have only two words for you," Andie said. "Pucker up."

Chapter 15

Sunday morning dawned bright and sunny. Fortunately, it had been a balmy, clear night the night before. Which was a very, very good thing, since Pacey and Andie still had their lips plastered to each other.

They'd been allowed five-minute breaks every hour, a fifteen-minute break every three hours, and two hours to sleep in their sleeping bags between two and four o'clock in the morning. Twenty couples had already thrown in the kissing towel, and only three couples were left.

Every time Pacey or Andie wanted to give up, Pacey looked over at the Viper parked under the big tent on the square, and he renewed his smooching resolve.

Now, at nine o'clock in the morning, Gale Leery was already there with a news crew, ready to cover the winning kissers for the local news, and hundreds of people surrounded the final three couples, egging them on and betting on the winners.

"My lips feel shredded," Andie mumbled against Pacey's mouth. They were sitting on their sleeping bags, trying not to fall asleep from exhaustion.

"Hang in there. You'll end up in the Girlfriend Hall of Fame for this, McPhee," Pacey mumbled back.

"Famous? Lipless!" Andie managed.

"Oh my God, ladies and gentlemen, they are still at it!" Dawson exclaimed, as he and Joey hurried over to them. "We just got here. Jen's around somewhere, with Drake. You mean you've been here like this all night?"

It was kind of difficult to talk, so neither Pacey nor Andie bothered to respond.

"Have you guys even eaten anything?" Joey asked.

"Lots of Power Bars and Gatorade," Andie got out.

Dawson made a face. "Can I get you anything?"

"Collagen injections," Andie said, changing positions.

Little Dina Wolfe sidled up to Dawson. "Hi, Dawson," she said, looking up at him coyly.

"Oh, hi, Dina," Dawson said. There were two girls with her, clad in skimpy halter T-shirts, who looked to be a few years older than her. They also looked familiar. "Do I know you girls from somewhere?" Dawson asked them.

The redhead grinned, flashing her braces, and

then Dawson remembered. "Ah yes, the Ice House," he said.

"I was the one who said you had a cute butt," the redhead reminded Dawson.

"How could we ever forget?" Joey asked.

"So, these girls are friends of yours?" Dawson asked Dina.

"Her mom knows my mom, so we hooked up," Dina said. Her eyes flicked to Pacey and Andie. "You know, Dawson, you and I could kiss way better than that."

"Call me when you grow up, Dina, okay?" Dawson said.

"But don't be in too big of a hurry," Joey added with a wink and a smile, remembering how she had once told Dina that growing up sucks.

Dina and her redheaded friend both gave Dawson what passed as their sexiest smiles and sauntered away.

"Hey!" Dawson yelped, spinning around. Dina had just pinched his butt.

"Kinda scary," Joey decided.

Suddenly, their attention was caught by the loud groan that burst from the college-aged couple kissing next to Pacey and Andie. The guy broke away from his partner's lips. "We're kissed out," he called wearily, falling back on his sleeping bag.

Gale Leery hurried over with her camera crew. "Bob Kelson and Allison Burr have just lost their lip-lock," Gale said, facing the camera. "How do you two feel?" She held her mike to the girl's face.

"I'm never kissing anyone or anything again as long as I live," the girl said.

Gale took the mike back and smiled into the camera. "Well, there you have it. Two couples are left in the kissing marathon, which has already broken the American record. The only question now is, who will be the big winners? Those of you who have been watching my periodic updates know that only our youngest couple and our oldest couple remain. Will it be Pacey Witter and Andie McPhee, high school sweethearts? Or Florence and Mervin Shervin, on their fiftieth wedding anniversary, who remind me that they did not marry that young, either? Stay tuned, folks. You won't want to miss it! From the Capeside Romance Festival, this is Gale Leery."

The red light on the camera went out, and Gale chatted with her cameraman.

Jen and Drake strolled over from the parking lot. They worked their way through the crowd and saw that Pacey and Andie were still kissing. Jen applauded them. "Now this is what I call tenacity."

Pacey and Andie mumbled inaudibly.

"It's just you and them," Jen said, eyeing the Shervins. "And you've got younger lips."

Andie looked over at the white-haired Shervins, who sat on twin lawn chairs, as they had all night. Their lips were still locked, but they both looked awfully tired, and Mervin kept nodding off while Flo made sure they kept kissing. They were so sweet. How could she and Pacey beat them?

It seemed positively un-American, or something.

Suddenly, Andie pulled her lips away. Pacey grabbed for her, but Leonard Thistle, a member of the city council who was serving as judge, came running over to them.

"The youngsters broke, folks! The youngsters broke!" Leonard cried.

"Andie!" Pacey sounded heartbroken.

"I—" Andie began.

"Too bad, kids," Leonard said, "but a great effort. Ladies and gentlemen, the Capeside Romance Festival is proud to announce the winning kissers, whose names will be recorded in the Hall of Records: Florence and Mervin Shervin!"

A festival hostess handed Florence a dozen long-stemmed roses. Another set red glitter–spackled crowns on Florence's and Mervin's heads.

As the news crew recorded the moment, the crowd cheered wildly, and some people helped Flo and Merv to their feet.

"Congratulations," Gale said. "How do you feel?" She held the mike to Merv's face.

"Eh?" Merv asked, cupping his ear. His crown fell off.

"We're a little stunned," Florence admitted, taking in the huge crowd of well-wishers and media people. "Mercy! But I just want to say that this is the best fiftieth wedding anniversary gift we could possibly have."

The crowd "aw"-ed and began to clap as Leonard led the elderly couple to the Viper.

"Can you get in the car for a few photos?" a photographer shouted.

The Shervins got in the Viper and smiled for the cameras.

"Tell me you didn't stop kissing me on purpose, McPhee," Pacey wailed.

"Well . . ." Andie gave him a guilty look.

"How could you do it?"

"How could I not do it, Pacey? Look at them. They're so sweet. They've spent an entire lifetime devoted to each other. Sure, they're not sophisticated or worldly. But they have each other. And that means they have everything."

Pacey groaned. "If they already have everything, did they really need my Viper?"

"Perk up, maybe they'll give you a ride," Andie said. She ran her fingers over her lips. "I'm terminally in need of Chap Stick."

"Threw in the towel, huh?" Dawson asked as he, Joey, Drake, and Jen crowded around them.

"Andie was overcome by octogenarian sentimentality," Pacey said. He looked over at the Shervins. Flo was behind the wheel and had started the engine, which she was now gunning with enthusiasm. "That's my car."

"It would only have been for a week," Joey reminded him. "And look how sweet the Shervins are. Can you imagine loving one person—and being loved by that person—for your entire life?"

"I can't imagine not, actually," Dawson replied.

"My car," Pacey said longingly.

"Cheer up, Pacey," Dawson said. "One day, you'll own a Viper, if that's what you want. And you won't have to return it after a week."

Pacey gave him a level look. "I realize, Dawson, that I have, of late, shocked everyone, including myself, by having actually studied for the occasional test and passing the occasional class. But the odds of eventual financial success on the level of, say, Viper ownership, fall somewhere between slim and none."

"You're wrong, Pacey," Andie said. "Don't you know that yet?"

He gazed at her.

"You are going to accomplish incredible things," Andie told him, her voice full of love. "Because you are an incredible guy."

"You make it extremely difficult for me to stay mad at you, McPhee." Pacey took her into his arms.

"That was the general idea." Andie lifted her lips to his, then stopped.

"On second thought," she said, "no kisses."

Everyone who had worked on *Don and Dulcie* sat together in the darkened high school auditorium as the final frames of their film played on the large screen on stage. Of the three finalists, theirs was the last to be shown.

As Drake/Don took Joey/Dulcie into his arms one last time, the camera pulled out to show the natural beauty of Capeside surrounding them. Then the film faded to black.

The audience burst into enthusiastic applause and Dawson beamed. Theoretically, no one knew who had made each of the films. The rules dictated that no credits appear, so that the judges couldn't be accused of bias. But everyone in Capeside knew exactly who had made *Don and Dulcie,* and as the crowd applauded, lots of people looked in Dawson's direction.

On the stage, as some people got up to stretch, the panel of judges huddled to select the winner.

Dawson rose and started pacing in the aisle. "I'm too nervous to sit," he told Joey.

"Dawson, there's no way in this universe that your film didn't win," Joey told him. "I mean, the *Look Who's Talking* takeoff with the babies giving a travelogue of Capeside was cute but wholly derivative. And the one with the sweeping vistas juxtaposed against watercolor paintings of Capeside, all set to classical music, was admittedly pretty, but what did it essentially mean?"

"Maybe the judges aren't looking for deep meaning," Dawson worried. "This all started out as a travelogue contest, if you recall."

"Hey," Drake said, as he and Jen walked over, hand in hand. "Listen, Dawson, I have to tell you, you really have talent, man. Your film turned out great."

"Thanks," Dawson said. "I appreciate that. You were great as Don."

"Well, I'm still, as they say, learning my craft," Drake said wryly, and then cocked his head at Joey. "But you rocked as Dulcie."

"And you," he pulled Jen closer, "are not only gorgeous, you're going to end up running a major studio one day."

"I like the sound of that," Jen decided.

"Hi, you guys," Andie hurried over to them, hand in hand with Pacey. "I'm so nervous. Aren't you nervous?"

"I keep telling her it's a lock," Pacey said.

"Thanks, but I don't quite see it that way," Dawson said. "Listen, whatever happens, I had a great time making the film. And the fact that all of you were so willing to give your time and your talent to it means a lot to me."

"Oooh, he's doing one of those post-third-act crisis speech things again," Jen winced.

"You really have to watch that, Dawson," Joey agreed.

"Uh, ladies and gentlemen," the mayor called into the microphone on stage, "if you would return to your places, I believe we have a winner."

Someone flicked the lights on and off, and everyone hurried back to their seats. A hush came over the crowd.

"First I would like to say again how gratified we were to have twenty-seven short films entered in our 'Capeside *Is* Romance' contest," the mayor said. "It was very difficult for our judges to select the final three that you saw this evening. So let's give them all one more round of applause."

The audience dutifully clapped, then quieted again.

"In third place," the mayor said, reading off a small index card, "is *Look Who's Talking, Capeside* by Heather Reese and Amber Goldner!"

As the audience applauded, two college-aged girls went up on stage, shook hands with the mayor, and were handed a certificate by the judges.

Jen was sitting on one side of Dawson, Joey on the other. At the very same moment, both girls reached for one of his hands. When they realized what they'd done, their eyes met.

Neither let go.

"For second place," the mayor went on, "we selected a very creative effort. The runner-up film is . . ."

Dawson couldn't breathe.

"*Don and Dulcie*, by Dawson Leery!" the mayor announced.

Dawson stood up, dazed, while the audience applauded.

Second. He had only come in second. No time capsule for the next millennium.

His feet led him up on stage, where the mayor shook his hand and handed him a certificate. He went to stand next to Heather and Amber.

"And, last but not least," the mayor continued, "the winner of the 'Capeside *Is* Romance' short travel film contest is . . . *A Picture Paints a Thousand Capeside Words*, by Florence and Mervin Shervin!"

"It can't be!" Pacey cried as the audience burst into applause. "It's a conspiracy! They're everywhere! When could they possibly have made it?"

As the elderly couple made their way up on stage, the crowd spontaneously jumped to its feet and cheered. The mayor shook their hands and handed Merv the winning plaque.

As Flo went to the microphone—she had to stand on tiptoe to reach it—the audience sat back down again.

"Mercy! Well, Merv and I want to thank you so much for this honor," Florence said. "We had always dreamed of making a film, you see. So we just parked our camper at that lovely campground just outside of Capeside and decided to make our dream come true. Oh, I should tell you that Merv did all the watercolor pictures." She beamed at him. "He has an eye for beauty."

"You can say that again," Merv yelled, pointing at his wife. With her voice amplified over the sound system, he had heard every word.

"Well, I guess you can see why he's always been my sweetheart," Florence continued, "and why he always will be. So thank you, Capeside, for giving Merv and me a romantic experience that we'll never forget. Capeside truly *is* romance."

The whole audience stood up again, applauding wildly. Even Pacey was on his feet, pounding his hands together, and Andie had tears in her eyes.

When Dawson came off the stage to join his friends, he was grinning wildly.

"You're not upset?" Joey asked him.

"I was," Dawson admitted. "But after hearing Flo's speech, how could I be? You can't argue with that kind of love."

Joey smiled at him. "No, Dawson. You can't."

Lots of people came up to shake Dawson's hand and to tell him how great his film was. His dad enveloped him in a bear hug, and his mother took some photos.

Some girls asked Drake for his autograph. Two even asked Joey, and she shyly signed her name on their official "Capeside *Is* Romance" souvenir program.

Drake turned to Jen. "They should be getting your autograph. Nothing happens without the producer."

"Especially a producer as good as you are," Joey said. Her eyes met Jen's. And they said it all.

"I was thinking . . ." Drake began, slipping his arms around Jen.

"What's that?"

"A sudden urge to see Los Angeles might overtake you at any moment."

"Whatever would I do?" she asked, laughing.

"You'd call me," Drake said. "And I would be one happy former soap opera actor looking for his next gig."

"Oh, look how sweet," Andie said, nudging Pacey in the ribs. "I think Jen really likes him."

"Yeah, that love thang is in the air," Pacey said.

"Oh, Andie, dear," a voice from behind her said.

Andie turned around. Florence and Mervin Shervin were standing there.

"Oh gosh, I'm so happy for the two of you!" Andie threw her arms around Flo, then hugged Merv.

"What a sweet girl you are," Flo approved. She wagged a finger at Pacey. "You be good to her, now."

"You can bet on it, Mrs. Shervin," Pacey said.

"Well, Merv and I just wanted to say good-bye. And thank you for being so lovely."

"Eh?" Merv asked.

"Mrs. Shervin—Flo," Andie said earnestly. "Before you go, there's just one thing I want to know. My parents, and the parents of just about everyone I know, I think, have all these problems making their relationship work. And . . . well, I'd just like to know. Is there some secret to keeping your love alive?"

"Eh?" Merv asked.

"SHE WANTS TO KNOW HOW WE KEEP OUR LOVE ALIVE!" Flo yelled. Then she looked at the crowd of teens. "Actually, there is a secret," she told them.

Pacey and Andie, Jen and Drake, and Dawson and Joey all waited to hear what Flo would say.

"Mutual respect?" Andie asked.

"Honesty?" Pacey said.

"Oh, mercy, yes," Flo agreed. "You must have those things. But really the secret is . . . marital aids."

Everyone's jaw fell open. Had she really said—?

"Eh?" Merv asked.

"MARITAL AIDS," Flo yelled.

"Right!" Merv boomed. "In a plain brown wrapper!"

"He's partial to the raspberry-flavored massage oil," Flo said sweetly. "Well, we're off."

The Shervins hugged each of them good-bye and toddled on their way.

"Andie, you can close your mouth now," Pacey teased her.

"I can't help it. That lovely little old lady—"

Pacey laughed. "Personally, I like her even better now than I did before."

"Me, too," Dawson agreed.

"Well, all I have to say is, I want to be loved like that when I'm as old as they are," Jen said. "Raspberry massage oil and all."

Dawson turned to Joey. "As Pacey would say, I am the amen corner."

She smiled her special, singular Joey smile at him. "You will be loved like that, Dawson."

"Is that a promise?" he asked hopefully.

"Let's call it a possibility," Joey decided.

And she slipped her hand in his.

About the Author

C. J. Anders is a pseudonym for a well-known young adult fiction-writing couple.